Two

Two Days Before Christmas

A Pride and Prejudice Novella

LEENIE BROWN

LEENIE B BOOKS
HALIFAX

Cover design by Leenie B Books. Images sourced from NovelExpressions and DepositPhotos.

Contents

Dear Reader,

> *On the following Monday, Mrs. Bennet had the pleasure of receiving her brother and his wife, who came as usual to spend the Christmas at Longbourn....The first part of Mrs. Gardiner's business on her arrival was to distribute her presents and describe the newest fashions.*[1]

The story you hold in your hand takes place in the intervening time between when Mr. Darcy and the remaining Bingley party members leave Netherfield and the day mentioned above when the Gardiners travel to and arrive at Longbourn for Christmas.

The reason I have chosen to highlight this quote is because while there might be a Christmas tree on

1. *Jane Austen. Pride & Prejudice (p. 73). Amazon Digital Services, Inc..*

the cover, there will not be one in this book, nor will there be carols or greenery or kissing boughs, for this book is not about the decorations of Christmas but the gifts — or more precisely, one gift, a gift of love given by a sister to a brother.

Chapter 1

Georgiana Darcy peered out her bedroom window to see who had come to call and was causing the flurry of activity in the halls. Her eyes grew wide as she saw her brother step down from his travelling coach and give some directives to a footman — likely about his trunk or possibly requesting tea. Those were the things he most often thought of first when arriving home from a trip. Her brows furrowed, and her lips pinched into a displeased pucker. Her brother was not supposed to be here in town. He was supposed to be in Hertfordshire with Mr. Bingley, learning how to be something other than unpleasant.

Honestly! It was her heart that had been broken by that cad Wickham, not his! Hers was mending, but his? She shook her head. If only she could do something to prove to him that, though she had been hurt — and grievously so –, her heart was no longer affected. In fact, she had recently begun to think that it had never actually been touched at all. She had not been in love with Wickham. She was nearly convinced of that fact. She had been in love with the idea of being loved, adored, and cherished by a handsome man. That she had not been and feared she might never be was what still caused a pinching pain in her heart. Her companion, Mrs. Annesley, assured her it was a foolish notion to judge every gentleman by the actions of one, but it seemed prudent to Georgiana to be cautious, just in case. She had been too trusting. No one could tell her otherwise. However, just because she needed to learn a lesson in prudence, did not mean her brother needed to continue to suffer. He had done precisely as he should. Her pain was not his doing. The fact that he still tormented himself with guilt was what made it nearly impossible for her to lay her own, well-deserved, shame aside.

She had spoken in confidence about such things to Mr. Bingley before he and her brother had departed for Netherfield, Mr. Bingley's new estate. He had promised he would do his best to see her brother engaged in activities that would bring him distraction if not pleasure. She had been so hopeful that Mr. Bingley had been successful, for Fitzwilliam's letters had been light in tone, sharing stories of the various people he had met and wishing he was free of the attentions of one particular person, Caroline Bingley. Added to that, yesterday, Mr. Bingley had called to inform her that her brother had done the most unusual thing by dancing with a Miss Elizabeth — the same Miss Elizabeth that had featured in more than one of Fitzwilliam's missives.

Why he was home when things had seemed so promising, she was uncertain. She grabbed a wrap for her shoulders and slipped her feet into her slippers.

"Your brother has returned," Mrs. Annesley said as Georgiana met her in the corridor.

"I saw his carriage," Georgiana replied. "It is very unexpected."

"It is," Mrs. Annesley agreed. "Do you wish for me to attend you?"

Georgiana shook her head.

Mrs. Annesley glanced down the stairs. "You will tell me how he is, will you not?" There was a note of worry in her whispered question.

As far as Georgiana was concerned, hiring Mrs. Annesley to be her companion was the best gift Fitzwilliam had ever given her. Mrs. Annesley's heart was far softer than her angular features and austere manner of dress suggested. She was also aware of far more than the spectacles that perched on her nose while she read and stitched might indicate.

"Of course, I will," Georgiana assured her.

A twinkle shone in the lady's eye. "Then be quick."

Georgiana giggled as she descended the stairs. Mrs. Annesley was quiet and reserved as was proper for one in her position, but she was also curious and lively when she and Georgiana were alone. Reaching the bottom of the stairs, Georgiana stopped and waited patiently as her brother removed his outerwear and apologized to Mr. Wright, his butler, for the unexpected change in plans.

Seeing her, he greeted her first with a smile and then open arms, which she ran into without a second's pause.

"I have missed you," he murmured against her hair before releasing her.

"You did not return on my account, did you?" Georgiana wrapped her arm around his.

"May I not wish to see my sister?"

His avoidance of her question was not a good sign. Such a tactic always meant he did not wish to discuss his reasons for something.

"You may wish to see her, but you should not do so at the expense of breaking your word to a friend." She felt his arm flinch. "Mr. Bingley called on me yesterday. He seemed eager to return to Hertfordshire." Again, his arm flinched.

"He may return anytime he wishes."

Her brows drew together. Her brother's tone was so flat, so uncaring — so very unlike him. "I assume Miss Bingley and the Hursts accompanied you back to town?"

"They did."

She lifted a brow and gave him an assessing look. "You know Mr. Bingley will never persuade Caroline away from town so close to the season. It was a struggle to get her to go with him at Michaelmas."

He shrugged? The only response she was going to receive to such a comment was a shrug?

"He will be disappointed," Georgiana said softly.

"That cannot be helped."

Georgiana's heart sank at Darcy's words. Mr. Bingley had been so eager to return to Netherfield and a particular lady. In fact, he had mentioned taking his mother's fede ring with him when he returned. Not returning would do more than disappoint Mr. Bingley; it would likely break his heart and the heart of the lady he had left behind.

"Now, as delighted as I am to see you," her brother continued, "I am desirous of a long soak in a hot tub of water." He gave her a tight smile. "To wash away the chatter of Miss Bingley."

He had not remembered to ask her if she was well. That was also odd. For the last several months, he had asked her that question at least three times a day and always upon returning from a time away. She released his arm but only to allow her hand to slide down and grasp his. "Fitzwilliam?" She waited until he looked up at her instead of at their joined hands before continuing. "Are you well?"

His eyes left hers and looked down the hall toward his room as he nodded. "I will be," he said as he lifted her hand and kissed her fingers. "I will be."

Georgiana pulled her lip between her teeth as

she watched him walk down the hall to his room. His shoulders were not as square as they normally were, and he ran his hand through his hair which was something he only did when thoroughly overwhelmed by a situation. He was not well. Something was most certainly wrong.

Georgiana gasped as a reason for her brother's melancholy came to mind. Unwilling to entertain the troubling thought for hours before she spoke to her brother again, she hurried down the hall and knocked firmly on his door. Then she waited. There was some shuffling in the room, but none that sounded as if a person were approaching the door, so she knocked again. This time she rapt so loudly that she was positive at least one knuckle would bear a bruise from the action.

However, her sore knuckles had produced the desired effect since her brother, minus his coat and cravat, opened his door.

"She has not trapped you, has she?" Georgiana demanded.

Her brother's brows drew together in question. "I beg your pardon?"

"Caroline Bingley. She has not finally succeeded in trapping you into marriage while her brother was gone, has she?" Georgiana's heart raced with trepidation. Caroline Bingley was not the sort of lady she wished to have as a sister, nor did she think her brother would ever be happy married to such a person. Caroline was not horrid, but she was not gentle or lively or particularly witty. She was just not the sort of lady Georgiana knew her brother needed for a wife.

Thankfully, shock suffused her brother's face as he blurted an emphatic no.

"You are not marrying her?" Georgiana asked again just to be certain of his answer.

"No, Georgie, I am not marrying anyone." The light in his eyes faded as he said it.

In spite of her concern for the sadness in his tone and expression, Georgiana smiled at him. "One day you will," she said hopefully.

"Perhaps one day," he replied without so much as a hint of conviction that it was true.

Oh, he was in a deplorable state of mind, and Georgiana was quite certain she knew why.

"Was there anything else?" he asked as he turned to close his door.

Georgiana shook her head. "Not at the moment."

"Then, I shall see you at dinner."

Georgiana stared at his closed door. "Perhaps, nothing," she muttered. "You will marry one day, and you will be happy," she declared to the door, "even if I must see to it myself." Having settled the matter with her brother's closed door, she turned and went in search of Mrs. Annesley. Undoubtedly, her companion would have some advice as to how to help Fitzwilliam.

For a full hour, between songs in the music room, Georgiana and Mrs. Annesley discussed Darcy's mood and the likelihood that he was denying his heart or worse — had been rejected by the woman he loved.

"Miss," Wright said as he stepped into the room. "Mr. Bingley is here to see your brother, but your brother is not available. However, Mr. Bingley is in quite a state, and I would very much dislike sending him away without him having seen someone."

Georgiana stacked her music and rose from her seat. "Thank you, Mr. Wright. Your judgment is always so good." She smiled at the long-time servant. "Mrs. Annesley and I shall receive him in the blue drawing room." She waited until Mr. Wright had left the room before turning eagerly to Mrs.

Annesley. "Mr. Bingley might be able to help us understand why Fitzwilliam is so dejected, do you not think?"

Mrs. Annesley exited the music room with Georgiana. "You must remember, that Mr. Bingley was not at Netherfield and that he has already given you his report about your brother's progress when in Hertfordshire. I would not be too hopeful, but I will not say that there is no chance that we might gather some useful information."

"A trace of something to help us is all I wish," Georgiana whispered as they entered the drawing room.

"Mr. Bingley," Georgiana said in greeting. "I do apologize that you must once again be satisfied with seeing only me, but my brother has just returned from the country and is washing away the remnants of his travel." She motioned for him to be seated.

Bingley sat down heavily in a chair, his arms crossed and a scowl on his face. "I know Darcy has returned since my sisters have also returned. What I wish to know is why he has returned."

Georgiana took a seat near him. "I would also

like to know that," she said as she smoothed her skirts and folded her hands in her lap.

"Did he not say?" Bingley asked in surprise.

Georgiana shook her head. "He seemed determined to avoid giving me any information at all."

"Huh," Bingley muttered.

"He was very unlike himself," Georgiana added.

"How so?"

"He seemed distant, almost cold."

Bingley rubbed his chin. "My sister declared he was pleased to have arrived in town and that she had never seen him happier."

Georgiana allowed her face to show her disbelief of such a statement.

"I had suspected there was some degree of exaggeration to her words," Bingley admitted. "He is not happy?"

Mrs. Annesley chuckled softly in her corner. "Pardon me," she apologized as she saw them both look at her, "but from what I saw and Miss Georgiana has told me, Mr. Darcy is very far from happy."

"Indeed?"

"Indeed," Georgiana assured him. She smoothed her skirts again and shot a surreptitious glance at Mrs. Annesley. "I was pleased to hear you had called for I am hoping you might be able to help us understand why my brother is so morose."

Bingley settled back into his chair. "I am not certain I can help, but I shall do my best."

Georgiana smiled.

"I shall call for tea," Mrs. Annesley offered. "And some of those little almond cakes you like so much, Mr. Bingley."

Bingley chuckled. "Thank you, Mrs. Annesley. You know how to make a vexed gentleman feel better."

"She is excellent," Georgiana whispered. "There is none better, of this I am certain."

"I would agree," Bingley whispered in return. "Now," he said, raising his voice, "what would you like to know?"

Georgiana tipped her head and arched a brow. "Your sisters are glad to be back in town?"

Bingley blinked. "Yes," he replied as if uncertain why Georgiana was asking such a question.

"Will you be returning to Netherfield?"

Again, he blinked and shook his head. "I cannot say. As you know, I had hoped to return, but my sisters assure me there is no need."

"No need?" Mrs. Annesley repeated as she took her seat once again. "What of the lovely lady you left behind?"

For the second time that day, Georgiana witnessed the light fade from a gentleman's eyes and be replaced with sadness. Fitzwilliam's distress, just like Mr. Bingley's, was, as she suspected, most certainly related to his feelings for a lady.

"My sisters assure me that she holds me in no particular regard."

Georgiana could hear how he tried to keep the pain of such a thing out of his voice. "Do you believe they are correct?" she asked gently.

He shrugged. "I am not good at judging such things."

"Most times," Mrs. Annesley added with a smile. "You are not a good judge of such things most times. It is the same with many men," she explained, "until a man finds a heart that beats in the same rhythm as his own."

He shook his head. "I am uncertain."

"Of course, you are," Mrs. Annesley agreed. "New experiences are always unsettling. I would not place my full trust and future happiness in the hands of another, Mr. Bingley. I would pursue my heart's desires until I had heard from the lips of the lady in question that all hope was vain. We are not all transparent with our affections. We can be as uncertain as any gentleman."

Bingley's brows furrowed. "But what if she smiles at every gentleman and not just me?"

"Then, she has a tender heart," Mrs. Annesley replied. "And it is likely that a tender-hearted lady fears being spurned more than others because she will feel it more grievously."

Georgiana knew there was truth in what her companion was saying. "I know there are those among my friends who would not feel the weight of a refusal as much as I have," she said softly and then shrugged. "Or perhaps they do feel it as much, but, rather than pain and sorrow, it is displayed as anger and viciousness."

"Quite true," Mrs. Annesley muttered.

"You truly believe I should return to Netherfield?"

"Yes!" Georgiana blurted. "That is," she continued, "if you still wish to see Miss Bennet wear that ring as your wife."

Bingley let out a great sigh. "I have no greater desire."

"Then go," Georgiana encouraged. "And invite my brother and me for Christmas."

Bingley's brows furrowed. "I do not think that is a good idea."

"Why?" Georgiana asked as the tea tray arrived. "Your sister will gladly go with you if she can be hostess for my brother."

"It is not that," he said as he took a small bite of an almond cake.

"Then what is it?"

Bingley swallowed his cake. "Your brother has told me of your ordeal in Ramsgate," he began cautiously. "There is a militia encampment in Meryton."

"I am not swayed by a uniform," Georgiana said lightly. "Nor am I swayed by pretty words any longer," she added more somberly.

"Wickham has enlisted."

Georgiana's mouth dropped open, and her eyes grew wide. "Oh," she said softly. A shiver of cold ran down her spine as she stood and walked to the window. She had hoped that when she heard his name uttered by someone other than herself, her brother, or Mrs. Annesley, she would be able to do so with more composure than she currently felt.

His being in Meryton would make going to Hertfordshire more challenging. It was not that she suspected she would be affected by him as she once was, but it was harder to forget the pain of rejection and your foolishness when faced with the source of both. She gasped and turned toward her companions. "Is he why my brother is so miserable?"

Bingley shook his head. "I do not think so. Although..." his left brow rose and his lips pursed as he considered the thought.

Georgiana's steps were quick as she returned from the window. "Although what? What might Mr. Wickham have done that has injured my brother?"

"We met Wickham on our ride one day. Neither of us expected to see him. I was not as affected by it as your brother was." Bingley paused.

"I know Fitzwilliam despises the scoundrel, as he should, but why would that make Fitzwilliam so miserable and only now, not while you were in Hertfordshire?"

Bingley tipped his head and shrugged. "That is the question, is it not?"

"Yes," interjected Mrs. Annesley, who was sitting forward in her chair, listening eagerly.

"Wickham was not alone," Bingley said

Georgiana took a tentative seat on the edge of her chair as things started to become clear in her mind. "She was with him," she whispered.

"If you mean Miss Elizabeth and her sisters, yes."

"My brother likes her, does he not? She was mentioned in so many of his letters, and you said he danced with her."

"As I told you yesterday, yes. I believe he has lost his heart to Miss Elizabeth."

Georgiana flopped backward in her chair, not caring that it was not how a proper young lady was supposed to sit. "She must have refused him," she said.

Bingley nearly choked on the tea he was drinking. "No, I do not think anything like that has happened, for I am certain my sister would have crowed over such a wonderful event." There was a note of sarcasm in his voice as he said the last part.

Georgiana sat forward again. "Then why would Fitzwilliam say he is never marrying?"

Again, Bingley nearly choked on his tea. "Never marrying? What?"

Georgiana shrugged. "That is what he said. I asked him if he had finally been trapped by your sister –"

Bingley guffawed. "Oh, he must be in a terrible state if you thought to ask him that!"

"He is," Mrs. Annesley assured Bingley.

Georgiana nodded her agreement as she continued. "He assured me that nothing so horrid had happened and told me that he was never marrying. Of course, I replied that he would someday, and he replied with a perhaps. A perhaps! My brother, who has always droned on and on about doing his duty and finding a proper wife, said he would *perhaps* marry! What?" she asked in response to the finger Bingley held up.

"A proper wife is not the same as a lady one wishes to marry," he replied. "Miss Elizabeth is a gentleman's daughter, but her father is of no great standing."

"So?" Georgiana huffed. Her brother could be far too particular at times. She understood following rules and meeting expectations was important but a gentleman's daughter was a gentleman's daughter. It was not as if her brother needed to marry an heiress or a lady whose father held a title.

He had said so many times when the subject of marrying his cousin Anne de Bourgh was broached.

"She has an uncle in Meryton and one in town."

"Many people do," Georgiana retorted. "I have an uncle in town — at least, I do when the House of Lords is sitting. And I have several uncles in the country who rarely come to town."

"Yes, but none of your country relations are solicitors and your uncle in town does not live near Cheapside, nor is he a tradesman."

"Oh." That made a bit more sense. A tie to trade was not something that all of her relations would appreciate. "It is her uncle not her father," she argued.

"So I have said," Bingley replied.

"Do you know the name and address of this uncle in town?" Mrs. Annesley asked.

Georgiana turned toward her companion with the same look of shock that Bingley was giving her.

"I thought we might call on her," said Mrs. Annesley. "To be polite and to find out a bit more about Miss Elizabeth."

Georgiana tipped her head. "Do you think it would be beneficial?"

Mrs. Annesley took a sip of her tea. "I do not know, but I would think it would be wise to perhaps caution Miss Elizabeth about some of the members of the militia. Only, of course, if it seems that the aunt is close to her niece." She placed her cup to the side and continued with a sly smile. "And it would not be such a bad idea to have some credible material about the fineness of Miss Elizabeth's relations — provided they are indeed fine people — with which to refute your brother's protests about why he cannot marry a lady he so obviously loves."

Chapter 2

The scheme was settled. Bingley would discover the address of the Gardiners and send it to Georgiana as soon as he was able. Then, she and Mrs. Annesley would pay a visit while out on a shopping excursion. Darcy, of course, was not to know about any of this. It was imperative that they discover the quality of Miss Elizabeth's relations before they attempted any sort of dissuasion of Darcy's beliefs.

Keeping her plans from being discovered by her brother proved to be far easier than Georgiana had expected it to be, for her brother either kept to his room, indulging in sleep, or sequestered himself in his study, pushing books around and consuming far more brandy than was his normal habit. While these actions made for much simpler scheming, it also caused both Mrs. Annesley and Georgiana to worry about Darcy.

He had taken a quiet dinner with them on Thursday, the day of his arrival, but it was not until Saturday afternoon when he once again made an appearance at any sort of table where food and his sister both were.

"I am thinking of returning to Pemberley," he said, taking a seat near the tea table that was laid out in the music room. "I see no need to tolerate the season this year. If we leave soon, we shall likely miss the worst of the cold weather, and the roads will still be passable."

Georgiana lowered her teacup to the table. This would not work! If he was at Pemberley, there would be no way to work on him to return to Netherfield and Miss Elizabeth. "If you do not wish to remain in town, Netherfield would be more convenient," she suggested.

He set his jaw and shook his head. "I shall not be returning to Netherfield."

"Not ever?" She asked in surprise.

"No. Never."

Georgiana recoiled slightly at his harsh tone. "I

apologize for my incredulity, Brother. I had thought you a gentleman of your word."

She rose from her chair, leaving her tea and sandwich behind, and crossed to the instrument. She could not enjoy her tea when her brother was threatening to unsettle all her hopes to see him happy. She leafed through her music.

"I shall ask Bingley to join us at Pemberley, where I shall be able to instruct him about estate management from the comfort of my own home."

She turned toward her brother. "You will teach him to manage your estate not his."

"An estate is an estate," her brother argued.

His arms were folded, and he wore that scowl which said his opinion was not going to be swayed. It was unfortunate for him that she was not willing to believe in the immovability of his opinion. His thinking was faulty — moulded and warped by emotions. She knew it was, and because of this, she also knew that with time and persistence, it was not entirely improbable that he would see his error. Had she not also, at one point, been swayed by emotion into believing a falsehood? And though it had taken the crushing blow of the revelation of Mr. Wickham's intentions to help her see her error, she had seen it and was better for it. The same would be true for her brother. She just needed to persist as strongly as she could until he saw how he was wrong.

"He will not come alone," she argued, hoping the dread of being confined to Pemberley with the Hursts and Caroline Bingley for an indefinite period of time would be enough to shake from his mind the foolishness of running as far as he could from Miss Elizabeth.

"Caroline will remain in town for the season. She will not leave."

Georgiana shook her head. "Oh, my dear brother, how mistaken you are! She has no wish to find a husband other than you."

Her brother shrugged. "I will not invite her."

Georgiana sighed. "She will manage to invite herself. You know she will."

"I know nothing of the sort."

"Then you are a blockhead," Georgiana said firmly. She knew that such a comment would draw his anger, but at present, something needed to shake him from his stubborn, morose state of mind.

"Georgiana!"

His tone was harsh and scolding as she knew it would be. She wished to apologize immediately. It was not like her to call her brother names. However, no matter how wrong it was or how red her face burned with shame, she would not retreat from attempting to make him see reason. "What else do you call someone who refuses to see things as they are. You know that Caroline Bingley has long desired to become your wife and mistress of Pemberley. In her three seasons, she has never entertained any gentleman in a fashion that would suggest she was looking for a husband — unless that gentleman was you! She hangs on your every word. She prances and preens to get your attention. She flatters and attempts to make me her sister." She blew out an exasperated breath. "I do not despise her. She is a friend of sorts, but surely, you must see what she is about?" She looked expectantly at her brother, who replied with a shrug. Georgiana rolled her eyes. He was so stubborn at times!

"Very well. Invite Bingley and see if his sisters do not both accompany him." She placed the pieces of music she still held on the piano and marched over to her seat. "I shall not like to live with you once you are married to her. I tolerate Miss Bingley quite well when we are together for a short duration, but I do not wish to be paraded about during my season by her." She blinked at the tears that unexpectedly gathered. Caroline was so very different from Georgiana. Caroline put herself forward. Georgiana did not, nor did she wish to be pushed forward in such a fashion.

"I am not marrying Caroline," Darcy growled.

"Do you truly think that you can survive a full winter at Pemberley without being trapped?" She wiped away a tear that had escaped her fluttering lashes and then took a trembling sip of her tea. "No," she said with a firm shake of her head. "I will not allow it. We will not be leaving town."

"You have very little say in the matter," Darcy retorted.

"If I might," Mrs. Annesley interjected and then waited to be acknowledged. "Miss Darcy's concern is not unfounded. A situation could very easily arise that would call your honour into question if the Bingleys were to travel to Pemberley with you. However, I believe the point to be moot. I understood Mr. Bingley to say he intended to return to

Netherfield when last he called. He seemed very determined to do so."

Georgiana wiped away a second tear and looked at her companion with trepidation. They had agreed that they would not tell Fitzwilliam of Bingley's plans until everything had been arranged.

"Bingley is returning to Netherfield?"

"Yes, sir. I do believe that is his intention." She smiled at her employer. "There is a lovely young lady who awaits him."

Georgiana's eyes grew wide, and she dared to glance at her brother. He was staring open-mouthed at Mrs. Annesley.

"But she is indifferent to him," he finally managed to mutter.

"Has she said as much?" Mrs. Annesley queried.

"No, but Miss Bingley and Mrs. Hurst assure me of its truth, and they were on friendly terms with Miss Bennet."

Georgiana saw her companion's lips twitch just slightly, and she waited eagerly to hear the point Miss Annesley was about to make.

"This would be the same Miss Bingley who insists her brother will marry Miss Darcy?"

"She insists what?" Darcy looked at his sister and then back at her companion.

Georgiana nodded. "Caroline has told me many times how well Mr. Bingley and I suit each other."

"I think," Mrs. Annesley continued before Darcy could form any more words, "that perhaps Miss Bingley does not wish to encourage an attachment between her brother and this Miss Bennet. I am certain that Miss Bennet's dowry and connections are not superior to Miss Darcy's."

"No, not at all," Darcy replied. "Miss Bennet is of little standing."

"That would not benefit Miss Bingley in her quest to rise above her roots, now would it?" Mrs. Annesley poured a cup of tea and placed it before him. "A gentleman does not know the heart of any lady until he has made an inquiry of the lady in question. Until then, it is all hearsay and speculation. Admittedly, listening to such accounts no matter their veracity will save a few from certain heartbreak, but it will just as likely doom many to misery, having given up their heart's desire without so much as a whimper."

Darcy eyed Mrs. Annesley cautiously over the rim of his teacup. The woman had come with impeccable references, and to date, she had proved invaluable to his sister, taking Georgiana under her wing as if she was a mother hen, pushing her out from the safe repose of her room and home when it was needed to advance her recovery, and instructing her in every necessary accomplishment she would require when it came time to make her debut. Surely, she was a lady whose advice was as good for him as it was for his sister, yet, he did not feel particularly ready to admit it. He did not wish to be rational and level-headed, for being rational and level-headed was precisely what had led him to leave Hertfordshire and reduced him to his current miserable existence. He could not remain in town. The temptation to return to Netherfield would be too great. The knowledge that she was so near and yet so unattainable would be agonizing. If there was a distance between them, he might then be able to forget her and her lovely eyes, pleasing figure, and quick wit. He indulged in silence as he drank his tea. Then, when his cup was empty, he placed it on the table and pushed to his feet. "Then, I will go to Pemberley by myself. I will send a request to Matlock House. I am certain Lady Matlock would welcome you to stay with her in my absence."

Georgiana's eyes grew wide and filled with tears, causing him to look away.

"You would leave me? At Christmas?" she whispered.

"Only because you refuse to go to Pemberley with me," he said, moving toward the door. "I will be in my study if you require anything or if you change your mind."

"When do you leave, sir?" Mrs. Annesley asked before he could exit the room.

He would be away at this moment if it were not for those blasted tears in his sister's eyes. His own sorrow somehow deepened at the thought of causing her pain. "Three, four days," he responded uncertainly. "That should give enough time for Mrs. Reynolds to prepare for my arrival." He turned toward his sister. "I will not send any correspondence until tomorrow."

She nodded but did not look up at him. The action was so reminiscent of how she had been following Ramsgate that he feared he was setting her progress back.

"I cannot remain in town, Georgiana. I just cannot." He gave a nod to Mrs. Annesley and, leaving the music room, headed to his study. He did not, however, reach his destination, before hearing a most unwelcome sound in the foyer. He glanced in the direction of Caroline Bingley's voice, hoping that she had not yet seen him and he might hide-away undetected. From the hand she lifted to wave at him, he knew he was not to be so fortunate.

"Mr. Darcy," she called.

He sighed and turned in her direction.

"I have come to call on your sister. She is such a dear, and I do dote on her," she explained as she removed her gloves and coat. "Louisa and I were uncertain if I would be so fortunate as to see you as well since my brother would not join us. He has been in such a foul mood since our arrival. He stomps about, slamming doors, and replying only in one-word answers. It is absolutely impossible to have a conversation with him about anything."

"He was not pleased with your arrival in town?" Darcy asked.

"Most decidedly not!" said Louisa. "I was thanking the heavens that I did not have to remain under his roof that first night." She shook her head and clucked her tongue. "Such a show of temper!"

Darcy's brows drew together. "A show of temper from Bingley?" He motioned to the sitting room in invitation to the two ladies. Bingley did not anger easily. He would become disgruntled at times and even cantankerous, but rarely did he become angry to the point of making a display. Darcy wished to rub the small pain that was developing between his eyes. His friend must have been even more attached to Miss Bennet than he had suspected.

"I do not jest," Louisa continued as she moved toward the room he had indicated. "I thought he was going to banish Caroline to our aunt's house."

"He nearly did," Caroline assured Darcy.

How he wished she would walk further away from him than she was. It seemed she always had to be within arm's length of his person — as if being there assured her the possibility of grasping him if he should attempt to disappear, which at this moment he wished he could.

"I should go get Georgiana," he muttered.

Caroline made a small sound of disbelief and favoured him with an amused smile. "Mr. Wright will see to it," she cajoled. "Darcy House only employs the best." She perched herself on a settee near his favourite chair.

He ignored her and walked to the window. "Your brother is truly put out?"

"He is!" cried Louisa. "Did he not seem so to you?"

"I have not seen him," Darcy admitted.

"Count yourself fortunate," Louisa continued. "He shouted about needing to learn estate management and how it could not be managed from town. Then he started in on how he had not taken proper leave of his new acquaintances and moved into something about servants who were depending upon him for their livelihoods. And then, he grabbed his hat and coat and flew out of the house saying he would speak to you and set things right."

"I was indisposed when he arrived," Darcy muttered. He had not thought Bingley would be quite so distraught about his neighbours and servants. Letters could be sent to neighbours, and servants could be kept on. It was not as if Bingley had to be there for them to go about their duties. Both Pemberley and Darcy House still employed staff even when their master was not in residence. It was not the same as employing a worker in a mill or shop who only worked when the place of business was open. "And he would not come with you today?"

"He is rather put out," said Louisa.

Darcy leaned against the window frame. Hopefully, he had not lost a dear friend. That thought was just as jarring as the tears he had witnessed in his sister's eyes a few moments ago. He shook his head. Apparently, he had made a rather large mess of things.

"He was growing far too attached to the area," said Caroline. "We have done him a service in separating him from it. The neighbourhood was not fit for one such as he. If we had remained, he would likely become just as repugnant as the rest."

Darcy tilted his head and studied Caroline. She was looking very pleased with herself. "Not everyone was distasteful. I remember you and Mrs. Hurst found Miss Bennet to be to your liking."

Caroline tittered. "She was the most superior lady in the area, but that does not mean she is to be our equal."

Darcy's brows furrowed. Miss Bennet was a gentleman's daughter, and as such, she was not Caroline's equal but rather outranked her.

"And our brother can surely do better than a penniless country nobody," Caroline added. "No matter how prettily she smiles."

"I suppose you are correct," Darcy muttered uneasily. He had disparaged Miss Bennet and her connections as readily as Caroline when he was convincing himself that removal from Netherfield was necessary, but hearing Caroline speaking now, it struck him how very arrogant it sounded. Again, he considered just what sort of muddle he had created.

"You said just as much, did you not?" Louisa asked.

Darcy nodded. Bingley had the wealth to attract a greater connection, that much was true. However, having spent the last two days in agony, attempting to rid his heart of its desire for a lady who did not even smile at him as Miss Bennet did Bingley, he was beginning to rethink his assessment. He rubbed that pounding place between his eyes. There was no reconciling his heart and his head while here in town. He needed peace and quiet and days of roads between him and Hertfordshire to accomplish such a task.

"I cannot see how a gentleman's daughter is not good enough," said Georgiana, who had just entered the room during the last exchange.

"Georgiana," Darcy cautioned.

She raised a brow and flipped her head. "Why I am only a gentleman's daughter," she said as she took a seat.

"But a wealthy one," said Louisa, "and with relations that are titled."

Georgiana shrugged and fixed her brother with a piercing stare. "Then I suppose I shall have to be content to be sold to the gentleman most in need of my wealth and standing no matter where my heart might lie."

"Georgiana," Darcy scolded. "That is not what was said."

"Was it not?" She fluttered her lashes at him, gave him a small smile, and said, "Then, I do apologize," before turning from him and, to his great annoyance, ignoring him as much as she was able for the remainder of Caroline and Louisa's call.

"Georgiana," Darcy called as his sister passed the door to his study later that day.

Georgiana took four more steps before stopping and abandoning her plan to ignore his summons. There was no need to stir his ire any further; he was likely angry enough with her for her recent behaviour. She had not seen him scowl as much as he had during Caroline and Louisa's call in a very long time.

"You wished to see me?" she asked from the doorway.

"Come in and sit down." He leaned back in his chair and waited for her to comply. "Your behavior today was quite disturbing."

Georgiana bit her lower lip and lowered her gaze to her hands.

"It is completely unacceptable for you to speak as you did — and in front of guests!" He rose and came to stand before her. "It was disrespectful. I expect so much more from you. Where have I erred?"

Georgiana peeked up at him. He was propped against his desk with his arms folded across his chest, looking down at her with such a sad expression that it nearly destroyed her determination to press her point. However, if she truly wished to see that heartbroken look in his eyes removed forever, she must not waiver. Therefore, looking down once again at her hands, which were nervously twisting in her lap, she answered. "Our parents, as well as you yourself, have taught me that a Darcy's word is to be steadfast. I am to consider promises carefully before I make them because a promise should not be broken save for the noblest of reasons."

"This is true," Darcy muttered.

Georgiana lifted her eyes to his. "That is where you have erred. You promised Mr. Bingley that if he leased Netherfield, you would spend the autumn and most of the winter seeing that he had things well-in-hand before Easter, yet you have come home and refuse to return to Netherfield for who knows what reason." She lifted a brow. "I truly do not believe it is to save him from a lady who is beneath him."

"None of that explains your behaviour."

"No, it does not," Georgiana agreed. "But it is my answer to your question. You have not erred with me. I know my behavior was wanting and drastically so. However, it seemed the best way to capture your attention and get you to listen to me." She stood and placed her hands on his folded arms. "You are my brother, and I love you with all my heart and hold you in the highest regard. You have cared well for me. You have even saved me from certain ruin. I wish to repay your kindness if only I knew how."

He pulled his arms out from under her grasp and opened them wide to her in invitation. Gladly, she stepped into his embrace.

"Let me love you," she whispered. "Allow me to care for you and point out your errors when I see them. I am not the foolish girl I once was." She lay her head against his broad chest and listened to him pull in a deep breath and expel it in a whoosh.

"We are all fools at times," he murmured as he squeezed her tight. "If there was a way for you to assist me with my current dilemma, I would gladly seek your help, but I fear there is not."

"You will not keep your promise to Bingley?" she asked quietly.

He sighed. "Your point was valid. I shall consider it."

"Are you still leaving?"

His grip on her tightened. "I do not know. I long to leave, to be far away from..." his voice trailed off and the room was silent for half a minute. "I will consider staying, but I cannot promise beyond that."

"I am sorry," she said.

"You are forgiven," he replied.

She shook her head as he released her. "Not just for my behaviour."

"Then what?" he asked as she moved toward the door.

"That I could not save your heart from breaking." She smiled a sad, knowing smile at him as she said the words that he had repeated to her over and over again after her ordeal with Wickham. He stood quietly, looking at her as if he was uncertain if he should acknowledge that what she had said was true or false. "It is in your eyes, Fitzwilliam. Your heartache is in your eyes," she whispered and took her leave.

Chapter 3

"Are you ready?" Mrs. Annesley poked her head into Georgiana's room.

Georgiana giggled at the unmistakable note of excitement in her companion's voice. "As you can see," she replied, checking her reflection one more time in the mirror. She always wished to look her best, but today, she felt particularly nervous about her appearance. It was not often you presented yourself without an invitation to a person you did not know in hopes of gaining her assistance.

"You are the picture of propriety and elegance," Mrs. Annesley said as she stood in the open doorway to Georgiana's room. "Your green wrap sets off your hair quite nicely, and that hairstyle is very becoming." She waggled her eyebrows and tipped her head toward the stairs.

Georgiana giggled once again. Mrs. Annesley

had been surprisingly animated ever since they had laid their plan to see Fitzwilliam happy. Schemes, Mrs. Annesley had assured her charge, were her speciality when she was a girl. Often, she managed to conduct them without getting into trouble, but not always, which, she said was part of the thrill of it all. Of course, after such a confession, she had to remind Georgiana that schemes were really not the thing for a proper young lady who wished to keep her reputation spotless and her brother from scolding. However, it was allowable this once because the cause was a benevolent one, and apparently, it also helped the permissibility of a scheme to include one's companion instead of undertaking it on one's own. It had been rather entertaining listening to Mrs. Annesley go around in circles about their plan — lauding it one moment and cautioning the next.

"You look very respectable yourself," Georgiana said as she joined her companion in the hall. "The blue of your pelisse is just the perfect shade to declare you serious and austere, while the red trim on your bonnet adds a hint of dashing style that proclaims you are not retiring and should not be overlooked."

anyone about *him*," she whispered as she and Mrs. Annesley stood before the door to the Gardiner's home.

"You do not have to say anything if you do not feel it is right," Mrs. Annesley cautioned. "Only share as you feel comfortable."

Georgiana nodded and took a deep fortifying breath as the door opened and Mrs. Annesley requested to speak with Mrs. Gardiner. They waited in a narrow corridor while the housekeeper inquired if her mistress would receive them. There was a scurrying of feet above them and a calling from one child to another followed by a hearty and delighted giggle that caused Georgiana to smile. She could see a maid, sweeping ashes from the hearth in the room next to them, and once the noise from above subsided, Georgiana could hear her humming a tune as she worked. This seemed to be a happy home. That along with the tidiness and smart decor spoke well of the people who lived here.

"This way, ma'am," the housekeeper said, leading them into a cozy family sitting room rather than the more formal one across the corridor from it.

It felt odd to Georgiana to be welcomed by a complete stranger into the heart of where a family spent their time. Even in her friend's homes, she was entertained in the formal sitting room during calling hours.

"Please, be seated," a lady dressed in a modern and stylish blue morning dress and white cap greeted them. "It is such a pleasure to have a full sitting room."

"We appreciate your receiving my companion and myself," Georgiana said as she took a seat and glanced curiously at the other two ladies in the room.

"Miss Darcy, Miss Annesley, may I present my nieces, Miss Jane Bennet and Miss Elizabeth Bennet," Mrs. Gardiner said by way of introduction.

Georgiana's mouth dropped open. "Miss Bennet and Miss Elizabeth?" she repeated, looking from one Bennet sister to the other.

"Yes, that is who we are," said Elizabeth.

Taking note of how Miss Elizabeth's eyes danced with humor and her lips curled ever so slightly upwards, Georgiana gave her head a little shake of amazement. "You are just as he described," she muttered.

"I beg your pardon?" Elizabeth asked.

Georgiana started and, recollecting herself from her shock at seeing the very person about whom she wished to speak to Mrs. Gardiner sitting before her, flushed with embarrassment. "I do apologize, but my brother has written me so much about you."

"Mr. Darcy has told you about me?" Elizabeth asked in surprise.

"Yes, in each of his letters."

Elizabeth's brows furrowed.

"Oh, do not worry, he wrote only lovely things," Georgiana said in an effort to assuage Miss Elizabeth's concern, but instead of having a relaxing effect, her comment seemed to deepen Miss Elizabeth's confusion.

"Mr. Darcy?" Elizabeth's tone was one of complete and utter disbelief.

"Yes," Georgiana replied.

"Huh," was the only reply Elizabeth made as if she was at a loss for how best to respond to such news.

Georgiana looked at her companion, silently begging her to supply some direction in which to proceed.

"We must apologize for intruding on you when you have family visiting," Mrs. Annesley said to Mrs. Gardiner.

"Yes," Georgiana said with a small smile of gratitude. "It is perhaps a bit forward to call without any previous acquaintance, but I assure you we came today with a noble purpose in mind." Her heart began fluttering again as she considered the topic she was about to broach. As always happened when her heart began to flutter as it was, her hands followed suit and began to twist in her lap.

"Have you just arrived in town?" Mrs. Annesley placed a hand on Georgiana's while she asked the question of Miss Bennet.

"We arrived on Saturday," Jane replied.

"And was it a pleasant trip?" Mrs. Annesley asked.

"Yes, thank you."

"Will you be staying in town for long?" Mrs. Annesley gave Georgiana's hand one last pat.

"My nieces will be with us until we travel to Longbourn for Christmas," Mrs. Gardiner said as a loud thud was heard overhead. "I will be grateful for the assistance with the children as we travel," she added with a laugh. "We are expected in Hertfordshire two days before Christmas."

"Three weeks complete then. A very nice length of stay, is it not Miss Darcy?" Mrs. Annesley said with a delighted smile.

"Oh, indeed it is," Georgiana replied.

"We always enjoy our time in town with our aunt and uncle," Jane assured them as tea, and a plate of sweets was set on a small round table near Mrs. Gardiner. "Will you and your brother remain in town for Christmas?"

"Our plans are not yet formed," Georgiana replied. She thanked Mrs. Gardiner for the cup of tea, and then added, "I had hoped to convince him to take me to Netherfield with him so that I might meet you."

"Indeed?" Jane said in surprise. "I had heard he was not planning to return."

Georgiana's lips pursed slightly with displeasure. "Yes, I have heard that as well." She tipped her head. "Did he tell you he was not returning?"

"No," Elizabeth replied, "Miss Bingley informed us that she, Mr. Bingley, Mr. and Mrs. Hurst, and Mr. Darcy would not be returning."

Georgiana smiled. "Well, that does sound like

something Miss Bingley would do. She is very good at arranging things to suit her desires. However, I know on at least one count that she is wrong." She gasped. "Oh, dear. This is not good." She turned to Mrs. Annesley. "When did Mr. Bingley say he was leaving town? It was today, was it not?"

"Oh, my, yes. He is likely halfway to Netherfield by now," her companion replied.

"He was returning?"

Mrs. Annesley smiled at Jane. "Yes, my dear, he had a particular reason for returning, but I imagine since you are in town, he will not remain at Netherfield long." She placed her cup of tea on its saucer and balanced it on her knees.

"He was returning to Netherfield for me?"

Mrs. Annesley nodded.

Jane's brows furrowed. "But what of Miss Darcy?"

Mrs. Annesley chuckled. "Did Miss Bingley imply that Mr. Bingley was attached to Miss Darcy?"

Jane nodded.

"He is not," Mrs. Annesley said before taking a sip of her tea.

"Oh."

With that one word, for the second time since Mrs. Annesley and Georgiana's arrival at the Gardiners, a Bennet sister seemed lost for words.

"I am certain Mr. Bingley's lack of attachment to Miss Darcy was not your purpose in calling today," Mrs. Gardiner prompted.

"No." Georgiana placed her cup on the table beside the sofa on which she sat. "Although, your nieces and some information I discovered through Mr. Bingley are the reasons for our call." She drew in a breath. "It was mentioned to me that there was a particular gentleman who had joined the militia who is known very well to my family." She paused to give her heart a moment to calm.

"Mr. Wickham?" Elizabeth asked.

Georgiana nodded and glanced uneasily at her companion.

"You do not have to say anything," Mrs. Annesley whispered.

Georgiana shook her head. "No, I must," she replied to Mrs. Annesley before turning back to Elizabeth. "There are things you should know about him. Things that neither my brother nor Mr. Bingley would ever tell you." She blew out a breath. This was even more difficult than she had imagined it would be. "You must not tell my brother I have said anything. I will tell him eventually." She wished to stand and pace the room or flee it, but she did not. Instead, she twisted her fingers together tightly and continued. "He does not know we have come to call on you," she said to Mrs. Gardiner, "and he will, no doubt, be displeased when he discovers it."

She stopped once again and drew a calming breath. "I apologize, it is difficult to speak of one's foolishness," she said in explanation for why she was dabbing at the tears that had gathered in her eyes. "Mr. Wickham's father was my father's steward, and so I have known Mr. Wickham all my life. He was always kind to me when I was young. He would tease and tell stories, and he would occasionally sneak an extra cake out of the kitchen to share with me. To me, he was a trusted friend. Then, he left to go to school, and I did not see him for many years. His father died, and then so did mine." She crumpled her handkerchief in her hands. Her heart was beginning to slow its pace as she spoke. "I was not aware of the provision my father had left to Mr. Wickham or his refusal of the living at Kympton –"

"His refusal of the living?" Elizabeth interrupted.

"Yes," Georgiana replied. "As I understand it from both my brother and my cousin, Colonel Fitzwilliam — he shares my guardianship with my brother — my brother gave Mr. Wickham a generous sum of money in place of the living. I do not know all the details. My cousin told them all to me this past summer, and I remember some of them. However, at the time when I found them out, I was too distraught to commit them all to memory."

Georgiana looked down at her hands. "You see, until this past summer, I still thought Mr. Wickham a trusted friend. When staying in Ramsgate with my former companion, I happened to meet him again. I had not seen him in years, well before I began thinking of gentlemen as handsome." She could feel her cheeks growing warm. "He was very handsome and as charming as ever. It was a pleasure to stroll on his arm and talk to him of home and his adventures at school. I soon found myself fancying myself in love with him, so in love with him, that I agreed to run to Scotland with him and become his wife. I knew that my brother would never allow me to marry so young, but I was certain that Mr. Wickham was my one true love, and I was his."

Georgiana took a deep breath and lifted her eyes to Elizabeth. "He was not my true love, nor did he care for me beyond my money. My brother arrived unexpectedly, and when the truth of what I had planned was discovered, he vowed that should I elope, not one farthing of my money would be given to my husband. He would see that I was cared for, but my husband would get only me and naught else."

Georgiana could see the horror in Elizabeth's eyes. "It sounds harsh, I agree. I was furious with Fitzwilliam, and, after a time of tears in my room, I descended to the study to tell him that I did not care if he kept every bit of my money. I loved George and would marry him though I was penniless." She shook her head. "I can still hear Mr. Wickham's laugh and words as I pushed the door open and heard him talking to my brother. 'Take her without a pound to her name?' he said, 'I would not take her for less than twenty thousand.' When I gasped, he turned on me with a cold laugh and said 'Surely, you did not think I loved you, did you?' I ran from the room. I am not certain what happened after that." Shaking her head, she continued. "I was so foolish, so duped, and utterly broken-hearted, but I was saved from a life of misery, of that I am certain."

Silence reigned in the room for a full minute before Mrs. Gardiner spoke. "You poor dear," she said. "How horrible."

Georgiana gave her a sad smile. "I have not spoken of this to anyone besides Mrs. Annesley, my brother, and my cousin; however, when Mr. Bingley told me that Mr. Wickham was in Hertfordshire and had made friends with a lady my brother admires, I could not let that lady fall victim to his pretty words."

Chapter 4

Not knowing what to say or how to feel, Elizabeth sipped her tea slowly as she considered what she had heard. The way Miss Darcy had wrung her hands, flushed, and fought tears during her tale made it impossible for Elizabeth to brush the facts away as a fabrication.

She lifted her teacup to her lips and allowed the warm beverage to flow over her tongue and down her throat as she swallowed. It amazed her how Miss Darcy could share such a story. If it had been Elizabeth who had been duped by a cad and come so near to ruin, she would have had to have a very compelling reason to share it. She shook her head slightly before she took another sip of tea. Conversation swirled around her almost as freely as her thoughts twisted and turned in her mind.

There must have been a very compelling reason

for Miss Darcy to share such a story with a complete stranger. What had she claimed to be her reason? Elizabeth swallowed the last of her tea. Miss Darcy had said it was because Elizabeth was a lady Mr. Darcy admired and therefore, Miss Darcy did not wish to see come to any harm. Elizabeth rose without a word, placed her cup and saucer on the tea tray, and returned to her seat.

Could it actually be true that Mr. Darcy admired her? Elizabeth's brows furrowed as she attempted to reason away Miss Darcy's claim, but finally, she had to admit that, if Miss Darcy's story about Mr. Wickham was true, then presumably her comment regarding her brother's admiration was true as well.

She considered all that Mr. Wickham had told her. According to Miss Darcy, Wickham had not been injured by anything other than his own actions. The living had been refused. A payment made in its place. And Miss Darcy, the girl that he said was proud and cold was anything but! No wonder Mr. Darcy had looked so angry when he met Wickham and replied so harshly when questioned about the man. Mr. Wickham had attempted to seduce his sister! Oh, how wrong had she been? Had every word of it been a lie? Had she truly been so easily led?

"Mr. Wickham has not been harmed by your brother?" Elizabeth asked when the conversation about something lapsed into silence. She had no idea what topic was being discussed as she had not yet been able to attend to anything more than the troubling thoughts filling her mind.

Georgiana shook her head. "No, he has not. Mr. Wickham has been disappointed by my brother, but he has never been injured by him. Fitzwilliam has always treated him fairly."

Elizabeth nodded and slipped back into her reverie about the conversations she had had with Mr. Wickham. Oh, why had she not questioned his words more? Blind belief was not her normal wont. How eager she had been to hear someone speak ill of Mr. Darcy! And for what reason? To assuage her own wounded pride? To assure herself that she was indeed better than Mr. Darcy had declared? That in so doing, it could be confirmed that his character was wanting, and he was not the sort of man she should long to have notice her?

"I apologize for unsettling you." Georgiana had risen and slipped onto the sofa beside Elizabeth.

"It is startling," Elizabeth replied. "He spoke with such confidence."

"Mr. Wickham is very good at crafting tales. I should know as I was completely fooled by them."

Elizabeth looked at the hand that had taken hers and was squeezing it in a comforting fashion.

"I think," Miss Darcy continued, "that he succeeds because we, ladies such as you and I, are agreeable and friendly with a trusting nature."

Oh, Miss Darcy's words stung! If only she had been agreeable and friendly instead of intent on soothing her pride by hearing anything that would justify her contempt of the man who had injured her.

She shook her head. "No, it is not my goodness that granted Mr. Wickham his success."

She pulled her lower lip between her teeth and looked at the others in the room. She would rather not confess her errors to anyone but Jane, if even her. However, she could not deny the pangs of conscience that smote her as Miss Darcy attempted to reason away Elizabeth's culpability in believing Wickham's tales. Therefore, after expelling one breath and drawing another, she began her confession.

"It was my desire to find fault with Mr. Darcy that caused me to believe Mr. Wickham." Once again, she shook her head at her own foolishness. "Why I did not listen to Jane's cautions, I do not know."

She saw the furrowing of Miss Darcy's brow and the concern in her eyes and squeezed the young lady's hand that still held hers.

"That is not true. I chose not to listen because my pride was injured."

"Not without just cause," Jane interjected. "No lady's pride would be unscathed by such a slighting comment." She looked around Elizabeth to Miss Darcy and then to Mrs. Annesley. "It was at the assembly when the Bingleys had just arrived in the Hertfordshire. We were all eager to meet them, of course. It is not every day a new neighbour takes his place in our small community. The town was welcoming, and Mr. Bingley returned their fervour in kind. His sisters and your brother, however, were not as enthusiastic to have met our acquaintances."

"Mr. Darcy is not always comfortable in new surroundings," said Mrs. Annesley.

"No, he is not," Georgiana added her agreement.

"He had not wished to leave me, although, I assure you, just I did him, that there was no reason he needed to stay with me. He, of course, did not agree."

"I can understand that," said Mrs. Gardiner. "If my child had been through an ordeal such as you had, my dear, I would be in no hurry to be parted from them until I was absolutely certain they were recovered."

Georgiana smiled. "That sounds very much like his protest about leaving. However, he felt obliged, and I insisted he go. Fitzwilliam can be rather surly when he is forced to do what he does not wish, but that does not excuse rudeness, and you said he was rude, did you not?"

Jane nodded.

"Mr. Bingley suggested to him that he should dance with me," Elizabeth said, taking up the story where Jane had left off.

"Oh, dear," Georgiana muttered.

Elizabeth expelled a breath and closed her eyes for a brief moment before continuing. "Mr. Darcy turned, looked toward me and said 'She is tolerable, I suppose, but not handsome enough to tempt me.'" Elizabeth's cheeks felt as if they were on fire.

Those words still stung. She had worn her best dress and had her hair styled just as Jane had suggested because it was most becoming. She had hoped to make a good first impression, which was something that was not easily done when one was always compared to such a beautiful older sister. It was not a complete impossibility, however, and Elizabeth had felt she had succeeded that night. She had even been complimented on her looks by many in attendance. Yet, in spite of her efforts, the fascinating and handsome Mr. Darcy had dismissed her as if she were a faded pair of boots, only good for an occasional walk about the country on a muddy day.

Georgiana gasped. "How despicable! And untrue! Oh, he is such a curmudgeon at times!" she cried before she snapped her mouth closed and apologized.

"His words are most certainly untrue," said Mrs. Annesley. "You are a very handsome young woman, and I will be so daring as to say my employer knows it."

Elizabeth shook her head in disbelief. Mr. Darcy had time and time again studied her appearance with a lofty air. Was he not looking to find fault or to prove his words from their first meeting correct?

"I am sorry," Mrs. Annesley said in reply to Elizabeth skeptical look. "I am certain that I am correct. In fact, I will shock you further by suggesting he finds you handsome enough to tempt him into considering marriage."

Elizabeth's eyes grew wide, and a small sound of disbelief escaped her. "That cannot be. I am not good enough for his notice let alone his consideration as a wife!"

Mrs. Annesley's smile in response was very similar — annoyingly so — to the one Aunt Gardiner used when she knew Elizabeth was incorrect in her reasoning.

"Truly, you are mistaken," Elizabeth added. Mr. Darcy had made it clear beyond a shadow of a doubt that she was deficient, had he not?

"I will allow that I might be wrong, but I highly doubt it," Mrs. Annesley replied.

"Oh, she is not wrong," Georgiana added. "Even Mr. Bingley knows that Fitzwilliam admires you."

"It cannot be." Elizabeth shook her head. It could not be true, could it?

"You do not hold my brother in high regard, do you?"

Elizabeth's heart skittered and thumped. How did one answer such a question honestly without causing pain to a girl who so obviously loved her brother?

"Do not worry about offending me," Georgiana added as if reading Elizabeth's mind. "I would not like him much myself if he had said such a thing about me."

Elizabeth saw a curious look that she could not quite decipher pass between Miss Darcy and her companion, which was followed by a small nod of Mrs. Annesley's head.

"Would you be willing to give Fitzwilliam a second chance?" Georgiana asked. "He is not always as discontented and dour as he likely was when at Netherfield."

Elizabeth shrugged one shoulder. "I suppose I could." How could she say anything else? Miss Darcy was looking at her so hopefully. It would not be so bad a thing to attempt to like Mr. Darcy to keep from offending his sister. There was little harm in being civil after all, was there not?

"Excellent!" Georgiana cried. "I shall tell him

that I have met you, and if he does not flee to Pemberley, I will send a note inviting you to tea — all of you, Miss Bennet, Miss Elizabeth, and Mrs. Gardiner. I would be delighted to have such pleasant company for an afternoon." Though her mouth was open as if she were going to continue speaking, she did not do so immediately. Her brows drew together, and her expression became somewhat distraught. Then she shook her head and smiled. "I shall just have to find a way to deal with Miss Bingley if she arrives. All will be well. I hope."

Mrs. Annesley stood. "It has been a delight to meet you, Mrs. Gardiner, and your nieces."

"Yes, indeed it has been a pleasure of the greatest sort," Georgiana agreed.

The sentiment was echoed by Mrs. Gardiner, Jane, and Elizabeth, as was polite. However, Elizabeth's still befuddled mind was not certain if it was either a pleasure or a delight to have met Miss Darcy and her companion as it seemed she was going to be thrown together with a disagreeable, though handsome, man who supposedly and surprisingly admired her. But then, her mind contradicted, it had been an interesting meeting, and she had to admit she was curious to see Mr. Darcy at his home where he might be in a better humor. Added to that was the fact that she rather liked Miss Darcy and would like to see her again. If only her mind would settle on how to think and feel.

"I will send a note even if Fitzwilliam does fly off to Pemberley," Miss Darcy assured them and, with that, Elizabeth's guest, who had borne such unsettling news with her, was gone, leaving Elizabeth to ponder all she knew of Mr. Darcy in as much solitude as a sister and aunt would allow.

Chapter 5

Two days later, Georgiana poked her head around the door to her brother's study.

"Come," he said with a smile.

"I am pleased to see you have not gone to Pemberley," she began.

He shrugged. "I would miss you too much," he admitted. It was true. He had no desire to be parted from her for any length of time, and he knew that sending her to stay with Lady Matlock would not be helpful for Georgiana's state of mind. His aunt was well-intentioned and doting, but she was also fixated on making proper matches and sharing the latest and most scandalous news of the ton. In his opinion, neither would be beneficial to his sister after her recent ordeal — no matter what Georgiana might claim to the contrary.

Therefore, after a frank discussion about Miss

Elizabeth Bennet with his cousin, Colonel Richard Fitzwilliam, over a bottle of port and a game of billiards, he had come to realize that staying in town would be the best for all. Richard had assured him that running from a problem was not the most successful way of overcoming it. Instead, he suggested, Darcy should face and vanquish the problem. This last bit of advice had Darcy considering returning to Netherfield as he had promised.

If he could put Elizabeth from his mind for the next two weeks, then he could surely return knowing that he had merely been infatuated. That was *if* he could put her from his mind. If he could not, well, then a new strategy might need to be employed whereby he could keep his word to Bingley.

"You truly are not going?" Georgiana asked hopefully.

"No, I am remaining here."

"Good," Georgiana replied with a smile, eying a letter with familiar writing on it laying open on her brother's desk. "Is Mr. Bingley returning to town?"

Darcy's brows rose, and his head tipped to the side. "Why would you expect him to return so soon?"

Georgiana smoothed an imaginary wrinkle from her skirt. "Because Miss Bennet is in town," she replied without looking up at him.

Darcy stared at her. "How do you know that?" There was no way she could have read Bingley's letter. It had just arrived, and he had just finished reading it himself.

"I saw her," Georgiana answered, lifting her eyes to him.

"Where?"

"At her aunt's house," Georgiana swallowed and waited for him to reply, hoping that he would not raise his voice too much or worse speak in that low, sad, disappointed tone that always tore at her heart.

"In Cheapside?"

"No, Gracechurch Street," she replied. "The Gardiner's home is very nice," she added. "It's not large, but neither is it small. The furnishings are very tasteful. Everything is well-kept, and the servants seem happy. I suspect Mr. Gardiner is a very well-to-do merchant and no mere shopkeeper." She stopped her rambling as she saw his lips purse and brows furrow.

"Why were you at Miss Bennet's aunt's home?"

"To visit her, of course."

His eyes narrowed. "Why?"

"Mr. Bingley happened to mention that Mr. Wickham was in Hertfordshire, and I did not wish for Miss Bennet or her sisters to be tricked by him as I was." She held her breath. His eyes had grown wide, and his expression did not look pleased.

"You intended to tell a complete stranger about Wickham?"

"Yes."

"Georgiana." Darcy stared at her in disbelief. How could she be so careless with her reputation? He shook his head.

"Fitzwilliam, you know how he hurt me." She scooted forward in her chair so that she could be a tiny bit closer to him. "How could I allow that to happen to another if I had it in my power to prevent it?"

"But a stranger, Georgiana? How did you know she would not bandy your story hither and yon? The Bennets are not heiresses. They have nothing with which to tempt him."

"They are pretty," Georgiana replied. "Even a pretty maid is not beneath his notice, not that he would pursue her for her money, of course." Her cheeks flushed with embarrassment.

Darcy's eyes grew wide. "You know about that?"

"One hears things occasionally," Georgiana replied, lowering her eyes. "It was told to me to assure me that I had lost nothing in not being loved by Mr. Wickham. It helped me understand your disapproval for what it was — not a condemnation of him because he is not a gentleman but because he is a rogue. "

"The connection would not have been good either," Darcy replied, "but you are right, I worried more about your happiness and safety than about his standing." He blew out a breath. "And do you believe Miss Bennet and Mrs. Gardiner will treat what you have told them with care?"

Georgiana nodded. "As will Miss Elizabeth."

Darcy's brows furrowed. "You gave them permission to tell her?"

"No," Georgiana said with a smile, "she is also in town."

In town? Elizabeth was in town? Bingley had not mentioned Elizabeth being in town, only Miss Bennet. Darcy rose from his chair and paced to the window. He was not ready to face his trouble just yet. He had not had ample time to work at forgetting her. Perhaps he should go to Pemberley for a time.

"She is quite lovely," Georgiana said to him as he stood in front of the window, running a hand through his hair. "I can see why you love her."

He spun towards his sister. "I do not love her," he snapped. He did not love Elizabeth, did he? He was only infatuated with her blasted fine eyes and keen mind.

"Do you not?"

"I do not," he answered with little certainty filling his mind. In fact, doubt, great heaping amounts of doubt, was creeping in around the edges of his thinking. Love. Love would explain why rather than thinking of her less with each day he was in town, he had found himself thinking about her more, would it not?

Georgiana stood. "She is a gentleman's daughter, Fitzwilliam. True, she has relations in trade, but so does Bingley, yet you accept him regardless of what any of our relatives say. I do not know the state of your finances, but I cannot believe that, with as careful as you are about everything, Pemberley is in need of funds from a wealthy wife." She crossed to stand next to her brother, who was once again looking out the window. "Fitzwilliam," she said as she wrapped an arm around his waist, "do not sacrifice your heart."

"I am not," he said softly as he placed an arm around her shoulder and drew her close.

"Consider it?" she asked, looking at him with pleading eyes.

He nodded slowly. He would likely be unable to not consider it now that such a thought had been placed in his mind, and his sister knew it. He kissed her forehead. "I will consider it."

"Excellent." She gave him a squeeze and then released her hold on him. "You know she is actually quite beautiful."

"I know," he muttered. She was captivatingly beautiful.

"Then why would you say she was merely tolerable?"

Darcy, who had taken his place at his desk, started and looked up at her. How did she know about that?

"You hurt her, Fitzwilliam."

Darcy blinked, and his stomach dropped. Elizabeth had heard him. No wonder she had done her best to avoid all his attempts to engage her in anything other than an argument.

"You should likely apologize," Georgiana said. "Or, at least, prove to her you know how to be civil."

Darcy gave a sharp nod of his head. Being scolded by one's younger sister was not pleasant.

"Miss Darcy." Mr. Wright stood behind her at the door, "you have callers," he said softly.

"Thank you, Mr. Wright. Would you be so kind as to see that tea is arranged?"

"Certainly."

"Will you join us, Fitzwilliam?"

Darcy shrugged.

"It is not Miss Bingley," she whispered.

Darcy chuckled. "Then who is it?"

A look of pure enjoyment suffused her face. "Miss Elizabeth, her sister, and her aunt."

~*~*~

Darcy stared at the place where his sister had stood before she flounced out of the room. Flounced! He shook his head. Georgiana had actually flounced out of the room. She had not flounced or behaved so carefree for very nearly three-quarters of a year. He smiled as he rose from his chair. It was good to see that part of her personality returning. He straightened his jacket, patted his hair, and checked his neckcloth before exiting his study. He knew that if he was to avoid his sister's displeasure, he would have to make an appearance and at least greet her guests.

He walked the length of the corridor from his study to the drawing room slowly. He could hear the rise and fall of female voices engaged in pleasantries. He paused before he reached the door. Elizabeth was in his home. Here under this roof where he had imagined her being. He shook his head. His sister's scolding would be better than seeing that vision come to life. How would he rid himself of it once he had witnessed it? He turned and walked halfway back to his study before the pull of curiosity and the shame of cowardice compelled him to retrace his steps to the drawing room. Again, he paused outside the door that stood ajar, but this time, with one last tug at his jacket, he pushed the door open and entered.

He paused and stood like a mute fool just inside the door. Reality was even better than his imaginings. Green was a very becoming colour on her, and she was sitting in the very chair he had imagined she would favor. He wondered for a moment if it had been her choice to sit there or if she had merely taken the chair next to her sister.

"Brother." Georgiana waited for him to turn his attention to her. "I know you have already met Miss Bennet and Miss Elizabeth, but please let me introduce you to their aunt, Mrs. Gardiner. Mrs. Gardiner, this is my brother, Fitzwilliam Darcy."

Darcy turned toward the one lady in the room whom he did not know. He opened his mouth to give her his greeting but upon taking in her appearance, found himself lost for words. She was impeccably dressed. Even Miss Bingley would not be able to find fault with the lady's appearance, but that was not what had struck him about her. He gathered his wits. "Forgive me. It is a pleasure to meet you, but I feel as if I have already met you somewhere. You look very familiar."

Mrs. Gardiner smiled. "I have a twin sister, and we both resemble our mother."

Darcy was unsure why this information might clear his mind. So he waited expectantly for the lady to continue but before she could, his eyes grew wide with recognition as an image of a lady he had seen many times in his childhood flashed through his mind. "Mrs. Pettigrew?"

"Is my mother," Mrs. Gardiner replied.

"You are from Lambton?" Darcy asked with interest as he took a seat.

"Indeed, I am, although, very little of my family remains in Derbyshire. In fact, it is only my cousin, Mr. Cooke, who still remains. Both my sister and I have husbands here in town, and our brother is long since passed — a childhood illness not long after my mother died," she added in explanation.

Darcy slumped from his normal rigid posture. "I remember that year. Illness seemed to be everywhere at once."

Mrs. Gardiner nodded. "It did. Many families were affected. Mine, those of friends, yours." She gave him a meaningful and sympathetic look. "Your mother was a wonderful lady. She frequented my father's shop often and was always so kind. I was telling my nieces about her after your sister's call. Miss Darcy resembles her both in expression and kindness."

"She does," Darcy agreed with a smile for Georgiana. "There are few hearts that are more generous and caring."

"That is a testament to your care for her," Mrs. Gardiner said.

"It was my father," Darcy replied.

"I must disagree," Mrs. Gardiner said with a shake of her head. "Your father may have laid the groundwork, but if I am accounting years properly, when your father died, Miss Darcy was at an age that is a threshold from childhood with several tender years between then and now when she is on the verge of her presentation to society. You, sir, have done well."

Darcy bowed his head in acceptance of the compliment. He was not entirely convinced that he had done much to help his sister become the lady she was. He had paid for school and made certain he was home whenever she had a holiday, and he had now employed two companions to see to her final preparations for her debut — one, Miss Annesley, had been a very good choice, while the other, Mrs. Younge, had been an instrument in bringing Wickham and near ruin to his sister.

Just then, the tea arrived, and Darcy assisted the maid with setting up the table. "Thank you, Nellie," he said as the maid finished arranging the things she was carrying. She curtseyed and slipped from the room without a word.

"I had not thought to see you in town," Mr. Darcy said to Elizabeth when he had returned to his seat.

"And I had thought to see you still in Hertfordshire," she replied, raising one eyebrow. "It was a shock to the whole neighbourhood when everyone from Netherfield left so suddenly."

Though her tone was light and teasing, he could see her displeasure in the flash of her eyes. "It was a sudden decision," he replied. "Perhaps not thought out as well as it should have been," he admitted. "And you? I do not remember hearing you or anyone else speak of a journey to town."

"Must I publish my intentions to travel?" Elizabeth retorted. "One might have plans that are not known to the whole of an area."

"Yet, I am accused of a hasty departure that has caused some acrimony in Hertfordshire."

"Mr. Bingley had said he was to return."

"Which he has," Darcy replied.

"Yes, well, that is not what Miss Bingley's letter said."

Darcy blinked. "Miss Bingley's letter?"

"The one she sent to Jane on the day your party left Netherfield. It made it very clear that her brother was not returning."

Darcy shook his head. "I did not know." Of course, he should have expected that Caroline would have done something like that. That woman could not make a quiet, graceful exit if her life depended upon it.

Elizabeth's head tipped, and her brows drew together just a touch as she scrutinized his face. "Very well, you are acquitted on that count."

Darcy dipped his head. "You are most generous." A small smile accompanied the statement which seemed to startle Elizabeth. "I do hope you can understand my reluctance to be away from my sister and to be confined to Netherfield with Mr. Bingley's sisters."

The startled expression on Elizabeth's face grew, and he knew that he had most assuredly made a very poor impression on the lady who captivated his every thought. It was quite likely if he were to pursue her and offer his heart, he would have it handed back to him in short order and without ceremony. The thought did not sit well with him. He should count it a blessing for the knowledge of such a thing should make it easier for him to overcome whatever infatuation he had with the woman, but instead, it cut at his heart, causing him to once again wondered if his sister might not be correct. He might indeed be in love with Elizabeth Bennet.

"Miss Bingley would like nothing better than to be the next Mrs. Darcy," Georgiana said. "However, my brother would rather not have her as his wife."

Darcy gave her a disapproving look. These were not things of which she should speak in company.

"There are many that would like to be the next Mrs. Darcy," Mrs. Annesley added. "But, their desires and those of the good gentleman in question do not seem to match. But that is how it is in the marriage market, is it not? There are the pursued and the pursuers. Things can get jumbled. Feelings can be roused and crushed, or hidden for fear of rejection." She clucked her tongue. "It was not so different when I was young."

"Indeed!" Mrs. Gardiner interjected. "Matchmaking," she said with a shake of her head, "gone wrong is the reason my nieces have come to visit."

Darcy saw both Bennet ladies cheeks grow rosy.

"My husband's sister was not pleased when her second eldest refused an offer she considered adequate for Elizabeth."

"Aunt," Elizabeth cried.

"She has five daughters to see well-married," Mrs. Gardiner continued, ignoring Elizabeth completely. "It is understandable that she would be anxious about accomplishing her task."

"Oh, it is," Mrs. Annesley replied.

"Who?" The question slipped from Darcy's lips. He had not intended to ask, but the shock of Mrs. Gardiner's revelation had him sixes and sevens. Someone had offered for Elizabeth? She could right now be someone else's save for her refusal? Surely, it was not —

"Mr. Collins," Mrs. Gardiner said with a hint of amusement in her tone. "Not exactly the sort of sensible gentleman our Elizabeth would appreciate, but then my husband's sister is more hopeful than sensible at times."

"Mr. Collins?" Darcy repeated in surprise. "They would certainly not suit," he added.

"And why would we not?" Elizabeth demanded. "Am I so deficient as to not be worthy of an offer of marriage?"

Darcy could not contain the shock that such a question brought. His sister was not wrong in that he had hurt the lady beside him most severely. He shook his head. "No, having been admitted to your presence, I would have to say that only an idiot would find you deficient in any way. I meant that the match would be unequal. You are far superior to Mr. Collins."

"Well said, Mr. Darcy," Mrs. Gardiner said. "If only her mother could see that. However, she cannot. At the moment, all she can see is her hopes to have two daughters cared for have been dashed first by Elizabeth's refusal of a good home and then by Mr. Bingley's defection."

Darcy turned his gaze from Elizabeth to Jane, whose head was bowed and a tinge of pink stained her cheeks. Had he been wrong in assessing her feelings for his friend?

"So, Mrs. Bennet has sent them to me in hopes that one might express herself more clearly and the other might, by some miracle of grace, find a man willing to accept her." She held up her hand. "Those are not my words. I find nothing lacking in either of my nieces. A man could not do better than to marry either of them."

"Aunt," Jane pleaded quietly.

"Very well, my dear, I shall leave off." And she did.

The conversation turned to what sorts of activities the Bennets might partake in while in town. Darcy added a few suggestions that he hoped would be appealing to Elizabeth. She had nearly been another's? The way his heart had felt as if it would stop beating to hear such a thing was all the proof he needed that his sister was correct. He loved Elizabeth Bennet. Now, he just needed to decide what he was going to do with such information.

Chapter 6

Darcy paced the length and breadth of the library at Matlock House. It had taken him some time to find his cousin. He had not been where he was normally wont to be at this hour of the evening, but Darcy had finally run him aground.

Richard Fitzwilliam was not the sort of gentleman to be lounging about home when there were more interesting entertainments to be found in town. Yet, to Darcy's surprise, home was precisely where Richard was.

"Darcy," Richard greeted as he stepped into the library and secured the door behind him. "What brings you to visit and has you looking so..." he tipped his head and looked his cousin up and down, "unsettled?"

"She is here."

Richard looked around the room. "Who is here?" he asked.

"Miss Elizabeth," Darcy replied, dropping into a chair near the hearth. "She and her sister are visiting their aunt." He scrubbed his face with his hands. "Georgiana told them about Ramsgate."

"Georgiana did what?"

"I was not pleased to hear it either," Darcy assured him. "However, she insisted that she could not allow others to be fooled as she was if she had it in her power to prevent it." He was still surprised that she had shared the story almost as much as he was by her reason for sharing it.

Richard joined Darcy near the fire. "I suppose that is, at least, an admirable reason for doing so."

Darcy nodded his agreement. "I do not think we need to fear Mrs. Gardiner, Miss Bennet, or Miss Elizabeth spreading the tale." As she was leaving Darcy House earlier that day, Mrs. Gardiner had made a point of whispering a promise to protect the information Georgiana had shared.

"Mrs. Gardiner assures me that we all make mistakes when attempting to lead a child into adulthood." He shared a rueful smile with Richard.

"Does she have children that are grown?"

"No," Darcy answered. "I believe the eldest is six. She has been instrumental, however, in Miss Bennet and Miss Elizabeth's lives. As I understand it, they have often visited with their aunt, and she is a sort of confidant for them."

"And you said the eldest Bennet ladies are well-mannered?"

"Yes."

"Then, perhaps she knows of what she speaks."

Darcy shrugged. "Perhaps."

"And is that what has you in a stew?"

"Only partly," Darcy admitted. "I love her."

"I beg your pardon?"

"I love Elizabeth," Darcy clarified, "and I wish to marry her."

Richard laughed. "Last night you wished to avoid any mention of her name."

Darcy rubbed his neck. "I know, but when she called at Darcy House and her aunt said she had refused an offer of marriage...Richard, I thought my heart would stop beating and, though I have tried for the past several hours to rid myself of the feeling of needing her, I cannot. I simply cannot imagine her with anyone else, nor can I imagine my life as even remotely happy without her in it."

"I see."

"Am I being a fool?"

Richard shook his head. "No."

Darcy looked at him, hoping that his cousin would elaborate on his reply.

"What can I tell you that you do not already know?"

"Her family is ridiculous," Darcy said.

"And so is Aunt Catherine."

"Her father's estate is mismanaged."

"That is not Miss Elizabeth's doing," Richard replied with a smile. "Her father has an estate; that is the relevant point — she is a gentleman's daughter."

"But she has little to bring with her to a marriage."

"Besides herself," Richard countered. "Is Pemberley in need of funds?"

"No, but she will likely bring her younger sisters with her — all three of them, hoping to be thrown into the paths of wealthy gentlemen. Silly younger sisters." Darcy shook his head at the thought.

Richard grimaced. "That could be a problem, but is it great enough to require that you give up Miss Elizabeth to another?"

Darcy scrubbed his face again. "No. I have argued all these points over and over, and the answer is always the same."

Richard cocked a brow. "A fool does not put so much thought into a decision, does he?"

Darcy shook his head. "I suppose not."

"Then marry her. Claim some happiness for yourself."

"Darcy, I had heard you were here," Lord Matlock said as he entered the library through the door that led to his study. "To what do we owe the pleasure of your visit?" He tipped his head and surveyed Darcy from head to toe just as Richard had done.

"He's getting married," Richard replied.

"I am considering marrying," Darcy corrected. "I must convince her that I am worthy of her first."

Lord Matlock leaned against the mantle and looked at his nephew with raised brows. "Have you shown her your bank accounts?"

Darcy chuckled. "She knows I am not poor, but it seems character, rather than wealth, is of greatest importance."

"Then she shall love you."

Darcy shook his head. "I am afraid I made a very poor first impression."

"Ah," Lord Matlock muttered as he nodded his understanding. "Put your foot in it, did you?"

"Indeed, I did," Darcy assured him. "She has an uncle in trade and another who is a country solicitor." He might as well get the disagreeable portion of this interview over with straight away.

"And her father?"

"He has a modest estate in Hertfordshire."

"I see. She is not of great standing, and you are worried that I will not approve."

"Something like that, yes."

Lord Matlock tipped his head from one side to the other and back. "I will not say that everyone will approve, but as far as I am concerned, I trust your judgment. He has thought through every ramification, has he not, son?"

"He has dissected it thoroughly," Richard assured his father. "He has even attempted to change his mind by fleeing her presence."

Lord Matlock chuckled. "That rarely works."

"So it would seem," Darcy agreed.

"You love her, then?"

Darcy nodded. "I do."

"I am glad."

"You truly approve?" Darcy asked in surprise. He had thought there might be some argument about Elizabeth's being of no standing.

"Very much so. I have always wished for you to find someone to love and to love you in return. You need a woman, not a fortune, to wrap your arms around. Now," said Lord Matlock, "I should like to meet this young lady so I will wish you well on your quest to improve her opinion of you, and when you have succeeded, send word. I will deal with Catherine for you."

~*~*~

"You were out late last night," Georgiana said as she took a place at the breakfast table next to her brother.

"I was," he replied, filling his cup once again with tea.

After receiving his uncle's approval to marry where he thought best, Darcy had spent another two hours with his uncle and cousin talking and playing cards. Lord Matlock had waxed eloquent a time or two on felicity in marriage and seeing that an estate had an heir. He seemed most anxious to have a grand niece or nephew whom he could bounce on his knee and tell tales — he had mentioned that more than once as well. The conversation had not all been about marriage or the best way to grovel ones way into the good graces of an offended lady; they had also discussed more mundane topics including the new upholstery Lady Matlock planned to order for their travelling coach once the weather turned warm enough to gad about town in the barouche.

"You were not dressed for a soiree when you left."

Darcy chuckled at his sister's attempt to not ask where he had been while still expressing her wish to know the answer to that very question.

"No, I was not." His plate was empty, so he rested against the back of the chair and cradled his teacup.

Her brows furrowed as she applied herself to cutting her toast into points before topping each with a different jam — raspberry on one, strawberry on the second, apricot on the third, and what Darcy knew to be her favourite, black currant, on the fourth. With that task completed, she filled her teacup and added just a splash of cream.

"I was at Matlock House," Darcy finally said

upon hearing her small frustrated huff as she stirred her tea. "Richard was at home, as strange as that may be."

"Indeed? Is he well?" Georgiana asked with a laugh.

"He appeared to be, yes."

"Did you have a good time then?"

"We did. Uncle Henry insisted on playing Casino." Cards of any sort were a favourite pastime for Lord Matlock. However, he was not one to frequent gaming tables for any length of time at soirees or his club since he desired for most of his money to stay in his accounts. A small wager was acceptable to lose, but one must always know his limits. Darcy had heard these words from his uncle many times over the years.

"And did he win?"

Darcy shook his head. "Once or twice. He was far more interested in talking than attending to his cards."

Lord Matlock was not known for being subdued. Richard often said that his father could strike up a conversation with a horse and convince the animal to vote with him on the next bill that entered the house. It was a skill that Richard had inherited, and one that Darcy, at times, wished he possessed.

"Were there any stories of particular interest that might be suitable to relate to me?" she asked as she began eating her toast — strawberry first as was her usual fashion.

Darcy chuckled. "No."

Georgiana's brows rose. "Indeed?" she said with no small amount of curiosity.

"Indeed," Darcy assured her. There was no way he was going to share with his sister about the duties of a husband to his wife, nor was he ready at this moment to admit to her that he was indeed looking for a wife — a very particular wife — Elizabeth.

Georgiana sighed and returned to her toast. "Are you going out today?"

"I have not decided. I might call at Mrs. Verity's. I am not expected there until next week, but I do enjoy reading to the children." He was considering calling on Elizabeth as well and possibly inviting her to go for a drive or perhaps an evening at the theatre or on a trip to the museum. They were all things that he suspected she would enjoy.

"Mrs. Annesley and I are planning to finish a few projects."

He could tell by the way she was smiling that those projects included a gift for him. "Will you be working on them the whole day?"

"No," she replied before washing down her third toast point with her tea. "Mr. Martin comes for a dance lesson this afternoon, and I have not yet mastered that Bach concerto. "

Darcy placed his empty cup on the table and, leaning back, watched her as she finished her breakfast. She had not looked so happy as she did this morning in a very long time.

"What?" she asked when she noticed his observation. "Do I have jam on my chin?" she whispered.

"No," he replied with a chuckle. "You have a smile on your face and an energy about you that has been absent for some time."

"I assure you, Fitzwilliam. My heart is healing."

"So you have said, and I am beginning to believe."

She smiled at him. "I will be finished soon. Will you wait for me and escort me to my sitting room before you lock yourself away with your books and whatnot?"

"I would like that," he replied.

Georgiana popped the last bit of black currant covered toast into her mouth and took up her cup. Leaning back in her chair to enjoy the last of her tea, she watched her brother for a full two minutes before he began to squirm under her scrutiny.

"Do I have jam on my cravat?" he whispered.

She shook her head and then, swallowed the last warm drops of tea before returning her cup to its saucer and standing in preparation to leave. "No, just a smile on your face and a relaxed air about you that I feared was lost."

"It would seem," he said as Georgiana wrapped her arm around the arm he offered her, "that my heart has found its hope."

She hugged his arm tightly and rested her smiling face against his shoulder. "I am glad," she whispered. "So very glad."

Chapter 7

"We have just one more place to visit," Aunt Gardiner told Elizabeth as their carriage crawled through the streets of the city.

They had been seeing to errands all morning. Elizabeth had agreed to accompany her aunt while Jane had wished to remain at home with the children. Therefore, Aunt Gardiner and Elizabeth had had ample time to talk about many things. The chief topic of interest for Aunt Gardiner had been the gentleman who had called with his sister on Friday, Monday, and Tuesday.

"The orphan house?" Elizabeth asked.

"Yes, Mrs. Verity's." Aunt Gardiner sorted through her parcels to find the one that Elizabeth knew contained two shirts and three petticoats. "It is not much," she said as she found the correct parcel and placed it on her lap, "but it will be appreciated. Mrs. Verity relies not only on her own funds — substantial though they are — but also on the generosity of her friends to meet every need of her charges."

Mrs. Verity was a wealthy widow, who, having no children of her own, had chosen to use the money left to her by her husband to set up a house for orphans. Her intention was not just to give them a safe place to live, but to educate them in every area of life that might afford them a proper future, free of crime and filled with hope — at least, that is how Aunt Gardiner had described it.

Elizabeth had to admit she was curious to see what an orphan house looked like. There was nothing of that sort in Hertfordshire, and the idea of a lady running her own establishment and aiding the less fortunate intrigued her.

"Mr. Darcy seemed disappointed yesterday when you refused his offer of a drive in the park."

Elizabeth's reply was a tight smile.

Aunt Gardiner sighed. "He is a fine gentleman — handsome and rich — and quite obviously besotted with you. I do not know why you insist on repelling his every advance."

Elizabeth wished she had an answer for that herself — or at least one that did not show her in such a poor light. "I have been such a fool, Aunt. I cannot see him without being reminded of my shame."

"Pride is a dangerous thing, Elizabeth." Her aunt tipped her head and looked at her very seriously. "Apologize."

Elizabeth pulled the corner of her bottom lip between her teeth and winced at that one word.

"Oh, it will smart for a time, to be sure," her aunt continued, "but then, it will be done."

Elizabeth knew it was true. The proper thing to do was to gather her courage and admit her folly. "He will hate me," she admitted in a whisper.

Her aunt's brows rose. "And you wish for him to *not hate* you?"

"Yes," Elizabeth could feel her face turning red. "I believe I have wanted him to not hate me ever since the assembly at Michaelmas. I had hoped when I saw him enter and when his friend paid attention to Jane that he might consider me." She looked down at her hands. "But he did not." It was the first time she had admitted how much Mr. Darcy's slighting comment had humiliated her. She had managed until this moment to wrap that pain in indignation and anger.

"Oh, my Lizzy!" Her aunt reached across the carriage and grasped Elizabeth's hands. "Then let him love you now. He is a good man. Do you not believe that?"

Elizabeth nodded. "He does seem to be a good and kind brother."

"He cares very well for his sister," Mrs. Gardener agreed. "I know many who would not treat a daughter or sister with such care after making such a scandalous plan as to elope with a ne'er-do-well. Why, there is one young lady who found herself in Mrs. Verity's care after being caught with a beau of whom her father did not approve. Miss Darcy was not ruined as this girl was, but still, to be cast out in such a way." She shook her head. "And you know as well as I that she is one of the fortunate ones to have found a good place to live until she could find a position where she could earn her keep."

Elizabeth nodded. Everything that she had seen or heard about Mr. Darcy since she had arrived in town spoke of his goodness. "I am being foolish, I know."

Her aunt patted her hand. "Learning to love is a fearful prospect."

"Love?" the word jumped from Elizabeth's lips.

She did not love Mr. Darcy. She admired him; she found him attractive; she even found his company to be pleasant; but she did not love him.

Her aunt smiled as the carriage drew to a stop. "Yes, my dear, that is the opposite of hate."

Elizabeth's mouth dropped open and then snapped closed. "Just because I do not want him to hate me does not mean I love him. It means…it means…" she stammered indignantly.

"You value his good opinion," her aunt completed. "And when not having it can threaten to rend your very soul, then it is time to consider just how deeply you admire the gentleman. Do not be stubborn about this, Elizabeth, or you may lose something that cannot be replaced."

Elizabeth pressed her lips together and followed her aunt out of the carriage and up the steps to Mrs. Verity's door.

"Mrs. Gardiner!" A lady with dark hair, streaked with thin ribbons of grey, greeted Elizabeth's aunt as she and Elizabeth entered a spacious study. The walls were lined with book-filled shelves. There was a grouping of chairs near a hearth, and another pair tucked in a window alcove. At one side, a large desk stood before two more chairs. It was to these chairs that Mrs. Verity directed her visitors.

"I have some shirts and petticoats," Mrs. Gardiner said as she placed the parcel she carried between two neat stacks of papers on the desk. "This is my niece, Miss Elizabeth Bennet. Elizabeth, this is Mrs. Verity, the capable headmistress of this fine establishment."

"Oh, be seated," Mrs. Verity waved away Mrs. Gardiner's compliments and chuckled. "Your aunt is always attempting to swell my head even more than it is already swollen."

"I speak only the truth," Mrs. Gardiner retorted with a grin.

"Well, then, I shall leave that to Miss Elizabeth to decide," Mrs. Verity arranged herself in the chair behind the desk and picked up a paper. "This is the young lady who is seeking a position," she said, handing the paper to Mrs. Gardiner. "And this is the lad in need of an apprenticeship." She handed a second sheet of paper to Elizabeth's aunt.

"We instruct all our residence in every useful skill," she explained to Elizabeth. "Both boys and girls are taught to read, write, and do their sums. The boys practice various skills such as placing and removing things from a table without being a distraction, tying cravats, planting, caring for animals, working with their hands, and when an aptitude in one or another of these skills is noted, we attempt to find them a place where they can earn both a bit of money and experience. Master Riley shows an inclination to be very good with figures. He is not meant to work with his hands. He must work with his mind."

"My husband thinks he would do well with Mr. Crenshaw," said Mrs. Gardiner.

"He may lodge here if there is no place for him there," Mrs. Verity turned her attention to Mrs. Gardiner who assured her that all the necessary arrangements would be in place before Riley began any work.

"The girls, such as Miss Clara, are taught cooking, cleaning, tending to and instructing young ones, as well as stitching and the like," Mrs. Verity continued her explanation to Elizabeth. "Clara has a love for fashion and can ply a needle and thread with such skill."

"Mr. Gardiner will surely know of a mantua-maker in need of an assistant," Mrs. Gardiner assured Mrs. Verity. "I see that Miss Clara is also skilled at making bonnets," Mrs. Gardiner said as she continued looking over the sheet of paper she held. "Would she be inclined to work with a milliner?"

"She would indeed. Again, lodging is available here if required, but if a place can be found for her as well as Riley that provides living arrangements, then I can take in two new children."

Mrs. Gardiner nodded her head. "We will see what we can do."

"You always do," Mrs. Verity said with a smile. "Now, your niece has not been here before. Would you care for a tour, Miss Bennet?"

Elizabeth looked hopefully at her aunt.

Mrs. Gardiner laughed. "I dare say I shall not hear the end of her disappointment if we do not have a tour. Elizabeth is an industrious sort of young lady who might need a charity in which to be involved after she is married.

"And is marriage in the near future?" Mrs. Verity asked as she led them from the room.

"No," Elizabeth answered as her aunt replied "possibly."

Mrs. Verity laughed. "The hopeful aunt, but I

can see why she is hopeful. You are a lovely young woman."

Elizabeth blushed and thanked Mrs. Verity for her compliment.

"Is there a particular gentleman?" The headmistress of the orphan house asked Mrs. Gardiner.

"I cannot say," Mrs. Gardiner replied while allowing her eyebrows to flick in a manner that told Mrs. Verity that there was indeed a particular gentleman.

Elizabeth shook her head. "Aunt," she pleaded.

"Very well," said Mrs. Verity, "we shall pursue that topic no further. This room on your left is where the children take all their meals. After they reach a certain age, they are required to take their turns in serving — not just because they may someday be employed in a fine home, but because there is value in learning to serve others."

The room was furnished just as a dining room in a wealthy estate might be furnished.

"It is beautiful," Elizabeth murmured.

"I give them the best," Mrs. Verity said. "They must learn to work in such places as this, so they must be familiar with both sides of the room so to speak. Those who eat and those who wait." She led them down the hall and up a set of back stairs. "The children are required to use these stairs at all times unless descending for lessons. I will show you the classroom last." She led them through the halls, showing them this room and that and introducing each child she met to the ladies.

Elizabeth smiled and curtseyed in response to each polite greeting she received. It was evident that Mrs. Verity and her staff had taught the children very well, and from their clear complexions and bright eyes, they were all well-fed and happy.

After touring the upper levels, Mrs. Verity took them down to the storehouses and kitchen before returning to the floor on which they had begun their tour.

"There were two drawing rooms and a library when I first purchased the house," Mrs. Verity explained as she stood outside a closed door. "We have kept one drawing room for receiving guests, and the other two rooms have been converted into schoolrooms. This is the room for receiving guests," she said as she pushed the door open.

The room was empty save for a young woman sitting near the window stitching.

Elizabeth stopped and stared at the woman. She

looked very much like the maid who had delivered the tea to the drawing room at Darcy House. "Does she work here?" she whispered to Mrs. Verity.

"No," Mrs. Verity paused. "Not all of our children are orphans. Some, such as Nellie's son, are foundlings."

"Nellie?" Elizabeth whispered. It was Mr. Darcy's maid.

Mrs. Verity nodded. "She keeps her son here so that she can continue to work. A maid cannot care for a child and fulfill her duties."

"She has no husband?"

"No, she has never had a husband," Mrs. Verity said softly. "Maids can fall prey to the gentlemen of a house."

Elizabeth's stomach felt as if it had dropped to her toes. "And that is what happened to Nellie?"

"Yes."

The one word answer made Elizabeth blink at sudden tears. How could she even consider a man who would take advantage of one of his maids in such a way?

"How sad," she muttered, both because it was a dismal realization about the man she admired and because it was sad that a maid should be treated so.

"Indeed, it is. However, Nellie's employer allows her to visit regularly and be involved in her son's life. That is much more than most foundlings are ever given. Her son will be along to see her soon." She looked at the pocket watch which hung with several other baubles and keys on a chain around her waist. "Ten more minutes and reading time will be over, and Robert will be free to visit with his mother."

Elizabeth followed Mrs. Verity to the next door.

"As I mentioned before, the remaining rooms were made over into classrooms — one for the older children and one for the younger ones. The two rooms are connected by a door, and from time to time, the younger and older children learn together. She cracked the door open slowly, and whispered, "such as now. It is good for all ages to hear literature read aloud even if they cannot decipher the words themselves." She held a finger to her lips and did not open the door any further.

"*...And I have felt*

A presence that disturbs me with the joy

Of elevated thoughts; a sense sublime

Of something far more deeply interfused,

Whose dwelling is the light of setting suns,

And the round ocean and the living air,
And the blue sky, and in the mind of man:
A motion and a spirit, that impels
All thinking things, all objects of all thought,
And rolls through all things...."[1]

The rich, familiar baritone of the reader wafted into the hall, wrapping itself around Elizabeth's heart with a deep sadness that ran exactly opposite of the sentiments of the poet. She fought to maintain control of her emotions.

Mrs. Verity motioned her forward and pushed the door open just a bit further.

Elizabeth peered into the room, a dozen children of various ages sat attentively listening. Some sat on the floor, others in chairs, and one small boy with blonde curls snuggled into Mr. Darcy's shoulder. Elizabeth looked from that young boy to Mrs. Verity.

"That is Nellie's son, Robert," she whispered.

Her words snatched the air from Elizabeth's lungs. The room felt warm and her legs unstable. "I need a bit of air," she said, and quickly fled the

1. *from Lines Composed a Few Miles above Tintern Abbey, On Revisiting the Banks of the Wye during a Tour. July 13, 1798, by William Wordsworth*

sight of the man, whom she loved, holding his maid's son.

Chapter 8

Elizabeth hurried through the hall and out the front door of the house. She stood on the step and pulled in several deep breaths of crisp December air. The image of Mr. Darcy with that child nestled in his lap pulled at her heart in two very different directions. Part of her could not help but be charmed by the prospect of a man as tall and handsome as Mr. Darcy snuggling a wee one, but when she thought of how that child had come into this world, her stomach roiled. She had long abhorred the practice of some men to take mistresses or satisfy their desires without the commitment of marriage.

"Pardon me, miss."

A boy, who looked to be about eleven, stood next to her with a broom in his hand.

"Forgive me," Elizabeth said, stepping to the side so that he could continue his work.

"That part of the step is clean if you wish to sit down." The boy kept peeking at her as he worked.

"Thank you. I find sitting would be most welcome."

"Wait, miss," the boy said before Elizabeth could do more than step down a step and prepare to take a seat. "The step is as clean as I can get it, but I should hate to see you soil your dress." He shrugged out of his coat and lay it on the step with the interior facing upward. "Yellow was my mother's favorite color," he said as he returned to his broom.

Elizabeth pulled her shawl more tightly around her shoulders. It would have been far smarter to have stopped during her flight to gather her pelisse. "You remember your mother?" she asked the boy.

He nodded. "I was six when she died. Papa passed the year before."

"I am sorry," Elizabeth murmured. She could not imagine losing both her parents now, let alone at such a tender age.

The boy shrugged. "Rachel, she's my sister, and I were fortunate, I guess. My papa left mother enough money to care for us, and when she got sick, she brought us here. I have wanted for very little."

Save for the love of a parent, Elizabeth thought. "You have lived here for some time then?"

He nodded. "Nearly six years." He gave the corner in which he stood one last good sweep. "There," he declared in a satisfied tone.

The door behind Elizabeth opened.

"Is our guest well, Riley," Mr. Smith, the butler, asked as he stepped out.

"Are you well, miss?"

"You have seen to my comfort very well," Elizabeth assured him. "I shall not inconvenience you much longer. I only wished for a bit of air."

"You will continue to see to Miss Elizabeth?" Receiving a promise from Riley, Mr. Smith handed Elizabeth's pelisse to the lad and then closed the door.

"How thoughtful," Elizabeth said, accepting her coat with a smile. "And, now you may have your jacket back as well. I would hate to be the cause of you catching a chill." She rose and put on her coat. Then, she folded her shawl and placed it on the step. "You may sit with me if it will not get you in trouble," she said as Riley appeared to be taking up a position near the door to watch her.

The boy considered it for a moment and then, just as Elizabeth thought he might refuse, he joined her.

"You are not with the others listening to the reading," she said as Riley made himself comfortable. It might be easier to avoid her thoughts if she were to begin a conversation with someone.

"No, miss. I have my duties to see to, and I am not going to be here much longer, so I must learn here instead of in the classroom." He smiled at her. "I will not lie and say I would not rather be listening to Mr. Darcy read than sweeping a step."

"You enjoy reading?" she asked.

"Very much." His head bobbed up and down vigorously to emphasize his point. "Almost as much as I like adding numbers." A grin split his face. "The others think I am a bit daft for liking sums so much."

"Oh," Elizabeth said as recognition dawned on her. "You are Master Riley."

"Yes, miss."

"My aunt and Mrs. Verity were speaking of you.

I believe my uncle is finding you a place with Mr. Crenshaw."

"I am anxious to begin."

"Mr. Crenshaw is a very pleasant man, and his wife makes the best plum pudding."

"He is kind?"

"Very," Elizabeth assured the lad beside her. He might look eager to begin his life, but she could imagine there was at least a small amount, if not a large portion, of trepidation hidden behind his confident smile. Leaving what one knew was never an easy task. Trusting another to care for them and be a good, kind, and giving soul was equally as challenging. Her lips curled up slightly. That was how she felt standing on the precipice of change. She would have to place her trust in another or remain an old maid, listening to her mother's moaning about how unfortunate it was to have a daughter who had never married.

The boy glanced at the door behind him. "I hope he is as good as Mr. Darcy," he said wistfully. "Mr. Darcy is the best gentleman I have ever met," he added. "Do you know him?"

Elizabeth nodded. Her plan to avoid thinking about that gentleman seemed to be crumbling about her and was about to be swept away completely by the young man next to her.

"I had only been here for a year when I met him. I had met many gentlemen and ladies. They come to see Mrs. Verity and to look at us, you know," he said in explanation. "Sometimes they take one of us to their homes to work. But Mr. Darcy was the first gentleman I had seen bring a maid to us."

Elizabeth propped her elbows on her knees and rested her head on her hands with her face turned toward Riley. "Nellie?" she asked.

The boy's face lit up at the name. "Nellie," he said as he nodded his head. "She let me borrow her handkerchief to dry my tears and never told anyone."

"That is very kind."

"Oh, she is," Riley agreed. "She never once teased me for missing my mother, and she took care of my sister so well. Rachel was only two then and in the nursery, where Nellie worked until she couldn't."

"She couldn't?" Elizabeth repeated in confusion.

The boy next to her nodded his head solemnly. "I should not tell tales, but she was with child when Mr. Darcy brought her to us."

Elizabeth's stomach once again began to feel uneasy.

"She had never been in the city before."

"She did not work for Mr. Darcy?"

"No, she worked for him, but not here. At his estate." The boys face grew dark. "Some friend of Mr. Darcy had promised to marry Nellie, but he did not. He ran away as soon as he knew she was with child."

Elizabeth's eyes grew wide. "A friend of Mr. Darcy's is Robert's father?"

The boy shook his head. "He is no longer a friend of Mr. Darcy. Mr. Darcy would not tolerate such a rogue."

Elizabeth's lips curled up at the adamant disgust in the boy's tone.

"Nellie was fearful, of course, that she would get turned out from her position, but Mr. Darcy would not hear of it. He brought her here until Robert was born, then, when she was well, she was able to return to work but not at his estate. She was to stay in town so that she could visit Robert. Sometimes she comes on her own, and sometimes Mr. Darcy brings her."

Elizabeth sat silently next to the boy for several

minutes. Although her stomach no longer twisted, her heart ached. How wrong she had been once again about Mr. Darcy!

"Robert was sitting in Mr. Darcy's lap while he was reading, " she said when the silence began to feel uncomfortable.

Riley nodded. "He always does."

Again, the pair lapsed into silence.

"Mr. Darcy is a good man," Elizabeth allowed that portion of her thoughts to be uttered. Good, however, seemed to be too small a word to describe a man who would see to the welfare of his maid and her child as Mr. Darcy was doing. Nor was it an adequate word to describe a brother who cared so well for a sister who had nearly been ruined.

She blinked. Those blonde curls! A chill crept up her back and spread down her arms. Nellie's hair was brown, but there was someone who claimed to be a former friend of Mr. Darcy who had blonde hair that curled around his ears and at the nape of his neck. Oh! She had once again been made to think poorly of Mr. Darcy because of Mr. Wickham! She blew out a breath.

"Are you well, miss?"

Elizabeth nodded and then shrugged. "Master

Riley, what would you do if you had misjudged a person most severely and had both spoken and thought poorly of this person?"

"Is this person a friend?"

Again, Elizabeth nodded.

The young boys face screwed up as he thought. "Mrs. Verity would say to apologize."

Elizabeth expelled one more breath and rose from the step. "Then, I must apologize," she said with forced determination. Biting her lip, she looked toward the door to the house beyond which lay the person to whom she needed to address her apology. "A good man would forgive me, right?" she asked her new young friend.

Riley smiled and nodded. "If he is as good as Mr. Darcy he will."

"I pray you are right," Elizabeth replied as she gathered her shawl from the step. "Thank you, Master Riley. I have every belief that you shall one day be as good as Mr. Darcy." The boy stood a little straighter at her words and nodded his head in acceptance of the compliment before moving to open the door for her.

Elizabeth stepped into the foyer and handed her

pelisse to Riley who stood behind her, waiting to take it from her.

"Did you get enough air?" Mrs. Verity asked as she approached Elizabeth. "I meant to see if you were well, but Mr. Smith assured me that Riley was seeing to your needs."

"He did a very good job," Elizabeth replied with a smile for both Mrs. Verity and Riley. "He was most helpful."

"Your aunt and I were about to have tea in my study," Mrs. Verity said. "Would you care to join us?"

Before Elizabeth could answer, the drawing room door opened, and Mr. Darcy stepped into the hall.

"Miss Elizabeth," he greeted. "Mrs. Verity said you were here."

"And as you can see, I am. I was speaking with Master Riley outside." Elizabeth was glad she could blame the redness of her cheeks on the cool air so that her embarrassment could be hidden for a few moments.

"Master Riley is a good lad." Mr. Darcy smiled at the boy who was scooting past them toward the back stairs. Immediately, the boy stopped his progress and with a bow, thanked Mr. Darcy for his kind words.

Elizabeth watched him continue on his way. "He adores you," she whispered.

"They all adore Mr. Darcy," Mrs. Verity added. "He is a favourite. Now, shall I pour for two or four?"

Elizabeth drew a breath. "Might I be allowed to speak with Mr. Darcy?"

Mrs. Verity's brows rose, and she shared a knowing look with Mrs. Gardiner. "Is Nellie still in the drawing room with Robert?" she asked Darcy.

"She is."

"Then I do not see why you cannot speak with Mr. Darcy in the drawing room, and when you are through, there might still be a cup of tea for you in my study." She winked and patted Elizabeth's arm.

Chapter 9

Darcy held the door to the drawing room open while Elizabeth entered. "I did not realize that your aunt and uncle were the Mr. and Mrs. Gardiner who help Mrs. Verity with finding positions for some of her charges."

"I did not know it either until yesterday when my aunt proposed my coming with her on her errands today." She took a seat in one of the two chairs tucked into the corner of the room nearest the door and furthest from where Nellie sat playing with her son. "I was intrigued by her description of this establishment and readily accepted."

"Your sister did not join you?" Darcy asked as he made himself comfortable next to her.

"No, Jane had promised the Gardiner children that she would play with them today, and breaking a promise is not something one should do, especially where children are concerned."

"I could not agree more."

Elizabeth drew a breath and expelled it slowly in an attempt to quell the flutters in her stomach. "I wish to apologize," she began. There seemed no better way to get the ordeal over with than to simply begin without a long prelude or drawn out exchange of pleasantries.

Darcy's brows drew together. "For what?"

"I have thought and spoken very poorly of you. I judged your character incorrectly." She dropped her gaze to her hands. It was so difficult to look at the startled and slightly sad look on his face. She would be hurt if she had been abused as she had abused him. "I truly hope that you will not hate me," she murmured.

"I do not see how I could," he replied.

She lifted her eyes and gave him a sad smile. "I believed what Mr. Wickham told me about you. I thought you were arrogant and rude and deserved to be spurned, and so I spoke harshly about you to my friends and relations." Her gaze dropped once more to her hands. "It was wrong, but that is not the worst."

"It is not?"

She shook her head and searched for her handkerchief in her pocket. She was quite certain that she would not complete this part of her confession without needing it. "Your sister made it clear to me that I had been deceived in my opinion of you, and I have seen by your behaviour in the times when we have met here in town that you are not arrogant and rude. You are reserved and perhaps a bit aloof at times, but not improperly proud as I had accused you of being."

She shook her head. Oh, what would he think of her when she told him what she had believed about the child who was squealing in delight over something his mother had said.

"When Mrs. Verity was giving us a tour today, I was surprised to see your maid in this room. Mrs. Verity explained that Robert was one of the children in her care and the result of a gentleman at Nellie's place of employment using her badly. I knew she worked for you." Elizabeth's voice faded as her heart pinched and threatened to break at what she must confess.

"You thought I was Robert's father?"

Elizabeth nodded and then covered her face with her hands.

"You think so little of me?"

Elizabeth could hear the pain in his voice, and the tears that threatened began to fall. She had no voice or words, so she simply shrugged and shook her head. She did not think of him poorly, not now. His good opinion, for which she had longed since their first meeting, was something she knew she had lost forever. How could it not be lost after thinking something so dreadful?

"I see," he said as he rose from his chair. "Thank you for informing me before I made a complete fool of myself."

"Please," Elizabeth choked out. "Please, forgive me. I was so wrong, so very wrong."

"I shall consider it," he replied softly. "Nellie, Harris will see that you are returned to Darcy House."

"Please," Elizabeth begged.

"I will consider it," he replied again. "I need to think," he added and then quit the room, leaving behind a softly sobbing Elizabeth.

She had thought he was Robert's father? She had considered him the sort of man who would use a maid employed in his own service in such a fashion? Did she know nothing about him? Had his insult and the tales of that blasted scoundrel blinded her to seeing anything of value in him?

He took his hat and gloves from the table near the door and, placing his hat on his head, stepped out onto the front step. He looked up the street and then down. Deciding that going up the street was perhaps the best place to find a hackney to drive him to who knows where — anywhere that she wasn't — he descended the steps and after a quick word with his driver, turned right and began walking.

He had not gotten very far before...

"Mr. Darcy! Mr. Darcy!"

He turned to find Riley running after him with a walking stick in his hand.

"You forgot this, Mr. Darcy," Riley said as he finally reached where Darcy was.

"Thank you, Master Riley," Darcy said, taking his walking stick from the lad.

"Mr. Darcy?" The boy called as Darcy turned to continue walking.

"Yes."

"A good man forgives, does he not?"

Darcy's brows furrowed. "Of course."

Riley nodded as a sad look crept across his face. "That is what I thought."

Darcy watched the boy walk back toward Mrs. Verity's. His shoulders were slumped, his hands were stuffed in his pockets, and he kicked at nearly every pebble which lay on the walkway. That was not how Riley normally carried himself. "Master Riley," Darcy called.

The boy stopped and turned toward him. "Yes, sir."

Sir? Darcy blinked. Riley used his name, not sir, whenever they spoke. "Are you well?"

The boy's chin lifted. "I am."

Darcy shook his head. "No, I do not believe you are." He took the few steps necessary to reach where the lad stood. "I have offended you in some way. I can see it on your face and hear it in your words. What is it?"

Riley lifted his chin once again and gave Darcy a very imperious look for one so young. "A good man forgives, sir." He gave a sharp nod of his head. "If you will excuse me, I have duties which need my attention."

Darcy stood staring after the child. Being

scolded by a younger sister was nothing compared to being called to correct behaviour by an orphan who at one time worshipped the ground on which you walked but now hung his head in disappointment at your actions or lack thereof.

He trotted up next to Riley. "I just needed time to think," he explained to the child, "to sort through the thoughts in my mind."

"She was scared," Riley blinked back tears. "I told her good men forgive."

"Miss Elizabeth was scared?" Darcy asked. Now that he thought about it, she had seemed rather nervous when she had greeted him. Her eyes had not met his nearly as much as they normally did.

"Yes."

"Of what?"

"She was afraid that you would not forgive her," Riley replied. "Oh, she did not say it was you, but I could tell."

Darcy felt as if Riley had hit him in the gut.

"She thinks you are a good man," the boy said, adding a second blow.

"She thought I was Robert's father." Darcy was unsure why he felt a need to explain this to a child.

"But you are not, and she knows that now."

When stated like that by a lad of eleven, it sounded rather obvious.

"You did not know she had thunk any of those things."

"Thought," Darcy corrected. "I did not know she had *thought* any of those things." He shook his head and slowly expelled a breath as he looked over Riley's head to Mrs. Verity's. "She did not have to tell me, did she?"

"No, but, when she asked what she should do, I told her what Mrs. Verity always says when we do something that is not right."

Darcy's lips curled into a rye half smile. "Apologize?"

Riley nodded.

"It was good advice, and it is advice I should follow." He blew out a great breath. "You are a good lad, Master Riley."

"Thank you, Mr. Darcy." The boy ducked his head, and his ears turned red. "I want to be good like my papa and like you."

Ouch. If Riley's words before had felt like a punch, this new revelation was more like a piercing of a sword directly to Darcy's heart.

"Master Riley, I have no doubt that you shall be

among the best of men." He placed an arm around the boy's shoulders. "Is she still in the drawing room?"

Riley nodded. "She was when I left. Nellie was caring for her."

"Then she is in good hands, is she not?" Darcy asked.

"She is," Riley agreed.

"I'm going to tell you a secret, that my father told me," Darcy began as they approached the front of the house. "Good men make mistakes, and when they do, they make amends as best they can." He smiled down at the boy's upturned intent expression. "And making amends becomes even more important if the person you harmed is very dear to you."

A smile split Riley's face. "You love Miss Elizabeth?"

Darcy nodded. "But, that is also a secret. I have not told her, and I do not know that my affections will be returned, especially now." He looked toward the window of the drawing room. "When I first met her, I said something that was not nice, Master Riley. I was in a foul mood, and I allowed it to get the better of my tongue. I have not yet properly apologized for that either. I know," he said in response to Riley's horrified look, "I have been remiss. My sister has already reminded me to apologize, and yet, I have not." He removed his arm from around the boy's shoulders. "Wish me well."

"Mr. Darcy," Riley called to him. "She is a good lady," he said when Darcy turned back to him.

"She is," Darcy agreed.

"Good ladies will forgive, but," the boy's brows furrowed, "not always right away."

Darcy chuckled. "You are far wiser than you know." He gave the boy a small bow and continued on his way up the steps and into the house to offer both his forgiveness and his own apology.

Darcy placed his hat and gloves back on the table just inside the front door and leaned his walking stick in the corner. Then, after straightening the sleeves of his jacket and aligning the buttons on his waistcoat, he sucked in a deep breath, expelled it, and with a slightly trembling hand, opened the door to the drawing room.

Elizabeth still sat where he had left her, but Nellie knelt beside her, rubbing her arm from elbow to shoulder and back as she whispered to her. Robert had climbed up onto the arm of the chair and was patting Elizabeth's back. Darcy closed the door quietly, dug his handkerchief out of his pocket, and approached her.

Nellie looked up at him, displeasure clearly written on her face.

"I have considered it," Darcy began. "I would be a fool to not forgive you." He knelt before Elizabeth. "I only hope you can find it in your heart to forgive me." He placed his handkerchief on her lap as she raised her tear stained face to look at him. How he wanted to gather her into his arms and attempt to erase the pain he had caused! But instead of acting on his desires, he turned to Nellie.

"Thank you," he said.

His maid looked at him warily.

"I promise I will not leave this room until all is resolved," he told her.

Nellie nodded and rose from her position. Then, gathering her son, she retreated to the other side of the room, and Darcy returned his attention to the weeping lady before him.

"I am rarely rational where Wickham is concerned," he began. "However, that does not excuse my reaction. I was startled."

"And hurt," Elizabeth whispered.

"Yes," he admitted. "I would never use anyone as Wickham does."

Elizabeth nodded as she dried tears from her cheeks. "I know."

Her voice was still soft as if she feared that raising it would open a new wound or bring on more tears. The thought tore at Darcy's heart. "What can I say to make amends? I fear I have erred far more gravely than you. I insulted you at the assembly — a patent lie." He shrugged and smiled softly when her eyes grew wide. "You are beautiful," he whispered before continuing.

"I was disagreeable and standoffish while in Hertfordshire instead of friendly and welcoming as I should have been. My behaviour has been deplorable. I would not think highly of me either. Added to that, is the fact that I returned to town, intending to dissuade Bingley from returning to Netherfield. I judged your sister's attachment to my friend to not be as great as his to her." He shook his head. "Who am I to decide such things? Can you ever forgive me for such arrogance and rudeness? Can we, at least, be friends?" He held his breath as he waited for her to respond.

"You thought Jane indifferent?"

He nodded.

"You would have separated them?" Her tone held a hint of anger.

He expelled the breath he had been holding. It was perhaps too much to expect a ready forgiveness after the sins he had committed. "Yes. I told myself it was so my friend would not be injured."

"It is not because you despised my family?"

He grimaced. "I will admit that I find it difficult to abide some of your family, but that was not the reason."

Her lips twitched for a brief moment. "I find some of them difficult to abide as well," she admitted before her brows drew together in question. "You said you told yourself it was to protect a friend, but that does not mean that Mr. Bingley's welfare was your true reason for separating him from Jane, does it?"

Darcy sat back on his heels. "It was not my sole reason." He swallowed and allowed his eyes to lower from looking at her face to watching her twist his handkerchief in her hands. "You had stolen my heart, but you were not what I thought I should consider for a wife." He heard her soft gasp and lifted his eyes once again to her face. "I was wrong about that as well. I do not believe I have erred as much in the entirety of my life as I have in the past nine months. First, I nearly lose Georgiana, and then, because of my abominable pride and my foul temper, I have likely lost my chance at ever winning your good opinion, let alone your heart."

"You wish for my good opinion?" There was no small amount of incredulity in her voice.

"I do. More than I can ever describe."

Her lips curved into the most beautiful smile of delight he had ever seen.

"I have wished for yours since the assembly," she confessed, ducking her head.

"You have?" It was his turned to be startled.

"I have," she said, meeting his eyes.

"Then, might we begin again?"

She nodded.

"I am forgiven?"

Her lips twitched, and that teasing left eyebrow arched as her lips parted to speak.

"Riley assures me that good ladies forgive," Darcy said quickly before she could say anything.

Elizabeth laughed, the sound filling Darcy's

heart with hope that he might one day be able to claim her as his.

"Then, Mr. Darcy, I have no choice but to forgive you."

He grasped her hands. "If you had a choice and did not feel forced, would you forgive me?"

She nodded.

He expelled a satisfied sigh.

"Do you wish to have tea with Mrs. Verity?" he asked as he rose from the floor and extended his hand to assist her from her chair.

Instead of taking his hand as he expected, her hand flew to her face. "I must look a fright," she cried.

"Not to me," he replied. "Never to me."

She pursed her lips and cocked a brow.

"Very well, your eyes and nose are rather red, and your complexion is somewhat wan. However, I assure you that while my eyes might see those temporary imperfections, my heart sees nothing but beauty." He smiled at the way her face reddened at his words. "Be that as it may, I will see if I can persuade Mrs. Verity to allow me to bring you a cup in here."

Chapter 10

Elizabeth peered through the front window of her aunt's sitting room. It had been a week since she and Mr. Darcy had come to an understanding of sorts in the drawing room of the orphan house. Mr. Darcy, with Mr. Bingley at his side, had called at the Gardiners each day, and she had welcomed him most happily. Today was no different. Her heart skipped, and a smile spread across her face of its own accord as she recognized the carriage which was driving up the street. He was nearly here. She tucked her work basket under her chair, making sure the square of cloth she was embroidering with leaves and scrolls was well-hidden before returning to watch out the window for Mr. Darcy.

"I take it our callers are nearly here," Aunt Gardiner commented with a laugh. "To think that the man you criticized so thoroughly in your letters could make you flit about as you are!"

"I am not flitting," Elizabeth retorted. "I am merely hiding a gift."

"You are flitting," Jane assured her sister as she crossed the room to join her. "And I am certain there is nothing wrong with it."

"Oh, there is nothing wrong with it at all," said Mrs. Gardiner. "In fact, I am quite pleased to have you both flitting about my house in anticipation of your gentlemen's arrival." She also joined them at the window. "I am delighted that you have both found such wonderful young men to love and who love you in return. It will not be long until we hear the banns being read for you both. Of that, I am certain." She placed an arm around each girl's shoulders.

Love. The word had been playing in Elizabeth's mind for two days now — ever since Mr. Darcy had declared his love for her in that drawing room while she used his handkerchief to dry her red eyes and nose. Her aunt had hinted even before that that Elizabeth might be in love with Mr. Darcy, and Elizabeth who could not accept that fact then was equally incapable of denying it now. She woke each morning with anticipation of seeing him in her heart and closed her eyes each night imagining his smile, and the hour or so he spent with her each day was the best part of her day.

"We should likely not be gawking out the window when they arrive," said Aunt Gardiner as the carriage began to draw to a stop before the house. "Come, have a seat."

Jane did as her aunt suggested, but Elizabeth remained at the window until she saw him alight from the carriage. He stood for a moment in front of the open carriage door, looking toward the house. Seeing her, he smiled and lifted a hand in greeting, which she returned in kind. Then, as he turned to assist his sister from the carriage, she took her seat to wait for him. The wait was not long.

"You are looking well, today." Darcy said as he took his place next to her.

"Do you truly think so?" Elizabeth fidgeted with the seam of her dress.

"Yes, I do. I am correct, am I not, Georgiana?"

Georgiana laughed. "You are rarely incorrect," she said, "which is highly annoying."

He shook his head and held up a finger. "Ah,

but when I am wrong, I am grievously wrong." He glanced at Bingley and then gave Elizabeth a sheepish grin.

Elizabeth's cheeks grew rosy. "A trait we seem to share, although I do think I am, in all likelihood, wrong more often but in lesser degrees, punctuated now and again with an error of enormous proportions."

Darcy said nothing but his eyes flickered with amusement.

"See how wise he is to neither contradict or agree with my assessment of myself?" Elizabeth asked Georgiana.

"Another annoying trait," Georgiana assured her.

"Were you successful in finding what you sought this morning?" Elizabeth asked.

"Mrs. Annesley and I have crossed everyone off our list. Not an item remains that needs to be purchased for our Christmas celebration."

"You will be joining Caroline and me for Christmas at Netherfield, will you not?" Bingley asked.

"Indeed, I would not miss Christmas in Hertfordshire for all the world," Darcy replied.

"I have told Caroline that we are to give a ball

on Twelfth Night, which has made her nearly delighted to be returning to Netherfield to display her talents." The amused smile Bingley wore spoke to the truth of his sister's preference to not be returning to Netherfield at all. "Before I left Hertfordshire last, I promised Miss Lydia that I would hold a grand soiree." He clapped his hands. "We must invite your cousin, Darcy. He would add a certain something to our lot!"

"If you mean he will fill your home with copious amounts of tales, and there shall never be a dull moment, then yes, Richard will fill that role admirably."

"I have no doubt the good colonel will keep us entertained, but that is not the particular skill I had in mind." He gave Darcy a pointed look, allowing his eyes to flick to Georgiana for a brief moment.

"I shall be well, even without Richard standing guard." Georgiana crossed her arms and pursed her lips in displeasure.

"I know I would feel much better knowing your cousin was near, my dear." Mrs. Gardiner interjected. "That scoundrel needs to feel his disgrace."

The subject of Georgiana's travelling to Hertfordshire was one that had been canvassed several times before her brother had agreed that with all the festivities of the season, it was unlikely that Georgiana would have to be in Wickham's company for longer than a brief meeting on the street — if even that.

"I will ask him tonight," Darcy assured Bingley. "I would also feel better knowing he was there." He patted his sister's hand. "And not just for you," he said softly.

The conversation shifted to more mundane topics as tea was served. Then, as Mrs. Gardiner gathered empty teacups and insisted on the gentlemen relieving her plate of the remaining sweets, Elizabeth slipped out of the room and went upstairs to collect her pelisse and refresh herself before leaving for dinner — an engagement that made her stomach flutter and her heart race.

Half an hour later, as she exited Darcy's carriage in front of Matlock House, she was not entirely certain her heart would survive its wild thudding.

Georgiana wrapped an arm around Elizabeth's. "They will love you," she whispered.

"And even if they do not," Darcy said. "I do."

"As do I," Georgiana whispered, "and we shall not leave your side the whole evening."

Elizabeth drew a breath, summoning her courage to face whatever might lie beyond the threshold to Matlock House.

"Then, let us begin, shall we?" she said with a smile.

Her heart might still be beating faster than was its normal wont in anticipation of tonight's events, but it was simultaneously filled with a most welcome peace, knowing that both Georgiana and her brother would stand with her.

"So this is the lady that has finally captured my nephew?" A distinguished looking gentleman with dark hair, flecked with silver, stood just behind the butler as the Darcys and Elizabeth entered.

"My uncle, Henry Fitzwilliam, Lord Matlock," Darcy introduced as he removed his hat, gloves, and great coat. "Uncle, this is Miss Elizabeth Bennet of Longbourn in Hertfordshire."

As soon as she was free of her outerwear, Elizabeth curtseyed and greeted him with a *my lord*.

"I do apologize. I was far too excited to wait in the drawing room for a proper introduction." He extended his arm to Elizabeth. "Darcy has never brought a female dinner guest with him before who was not his sister," he explained, covering

Elizabeth's hand with his free one when she placed hers tentatively on his arm. "There is nothing to fear," he assured her. "We are delighted to meet you."

Elizabeth tried to take in the beauty of the entry hall as he led her the short distance to a grand staircase, where they left the tiled floor of the entry hall and ascended the steps to the first floor and a very pretty pale blue drawing room. Lord Matlock stepped into the room and cleared his throat, drawing the attention of all who were gathered there.

"May I present, Miss Elizabeth Bennet of Longbourn in Hertfordshire."

It was strange to hear herself presented in such a fashion. She had never before felt quite so dignified as she did standing there, on the arm of an earl, being introduced with her name and place of residence. At home, she was just Miss Elizabeth.

"Miss Bennet," Lord Matlock was continuing, "might I begin by presenting the only lady in the room that outshines you, my countess, Audra Fitzwilliam, Lady Matlock."

Elizabeth dipped a shallow curtsey as anything deeper, though proper, was prevented by her hand still being fastened to Lord Matlock's arm by his hand.

"And this," he said, leading her to stand in front of a very fashionable blonde, "is my daughter, Lady Elinor Fitzwilliam and next to her, my son, Charles Fitzwilliam, Viscount Wyndmere." Lord Matlock leaned closer to Elizabeth and whispered. "He has no viscountess, but we are hopeful." The handsome gentleman before her rolled his hazel eyes at the comment.

"My father is very improper, is he not?" asked the Viscount.

"Indeed, he is," Darcy answered for Elizabeth. Georgiana had taken a seat, but Darcy trailed along behind his uncle and Elizabeth.

"Are you following me?" his uncle asked with a laugh. "I promise I will take good care of her."

"I have no doubt of that," Darcy replied. "But I do not wish for you to seat her on the opposite side of the room from me."

A second gentleman, who shared the same hazel eyes and light brown hair as the viscount, joined them. "Mr. Hughes said our guest had arrived." He bowed to Elizabeth. "Colonel Richard Fitzwilliam at your service."

"Colonel," Elizabeth greeted with another shallow curtsey.

"Well, that is all of us," said Lord Matlock. "Now, I suppose I shall seat you where Darcy can be at your side before he becomes too impatient." He chuckled as he led her to a pair of chairs near Georgiana. "I should not put you in such an uncomfortable position as to endure my teasing, but I cannot tell you how delighted I am to have one of my children so happily attached."

Elizabeth's brows drew together.

"Oh, I know Darcy is not actually my son, but he is very nearly the same." He clapped Darcy on the shoulder and moved to take a seat next to his wife as his son while Colonel Fitzwilliam took a seat next to Darcy.

"My father," he tipped his head toward where Lord Matlock sat, "is not cut from the standard aristocratic cloth as most of his rank are."

Elizabeth glanced at Darcy as she nodded her agreement. She had expected a more reserved greeting from his family. "He seems very pleasant."

"He is unless you are an opponent in the House," Richard assured her. "This assembled lot is the portion of our family that is agreeable — although

Mother can be rather exacting at times," he added before continuing. "Our aunt, Lady Catherine de Bourgh is as exacting as Mother but far less cordial. However, my father is the head of the family, and Lady Catherine is too well-bred to cross him." He smiled. "He is perhaps the only person she will not cross."

"Indeed," Darcy muttered as he shifted in his chair. He would rather not speak of his aunt at present. This evening was progressing well, and he did not wish to sour it with thoughts of Lady Catherine. "Bingley would like to have you join us at Netherfield for Christmas if your mother will allow it."

Richard shrugged. "I will petition her, but I cannot guarantee she will be amenable to the idea. Does she realize you will not be in attendance at Matlock House this year?"

Darcy shook his head. "I have not mentioned it yet."

"Ah," Richard said as he nodded.

"Georgiana is going to Hertfordshire with me," Darcy added.

Richard's left brow rose, and his face grew grim. "Is not that scoundrel in Hertfordshire?"

"He is," Elizabeth said softly. "I believe that is why Mr. Bingley wishes to have you join his party."

Richard's features softened, and he winked at her. "Are you certain it is not to foist his sister off on me?" he asked Darcy.

Elizabeth's eyes grew wide.

"She has twenty thousand," Darcy replied with a grin.

Richard paused and rubbed his chin as if thinking, then shook his head. "No, not even for twenty thousand."

"You are both horrid," Georgiana interrupted.

"No," Richard retorted, "Miss Bingley is horrid."

Elizabeth's mouth dropped open slightly. Miss Bingley was not her favorite person, but to hear her spoken of in such a fashion was not pleasant. "I would not say horrid."

"Would you not?" Darcy asked in surprise.

"No," Elizabeth replied.

"Not even after she attempted to separate your sister and her brother?"

Elizabeth's eyes narrowed. "Very well, I will admit she is not my favourite person. However, I do not believe it is best practice to speak ill of another, even if that person is arrogant and disdainful, for you may find that you have done so in error." She cocked a brow at Darcy as her lips curled into a slightly sheepish smile.

He tipped his head, acknowledging he understood of what she spoke. "You are correct, of course."

"But you are not the son of an earl or a wealthy landowner," Richard pursued the topic. "You have no idea how disagreeable it is to be pursued by one such as Caroline Bingley."

Elizabeth tipped her head and studied Richard's face. "Do you mind it so much?" she asked.

"Yes," he retorted.

Elizabeth, who was beginning to feel quite at ease, shrugged. "I will allow it to be true."

"You do not believe me?"

"My belief or disbelief does not prove your words true or false," she replied.

Richard laughed. "I can see why Darcy is enchanted. You argue very well, but do you not believe that being pursued for your name or fortune is unpleasant?"

"I believe, Colonel, that to be pursued for title or wealth is just as disagreeable as being cast aside for lack of either."

"I did not say I am casting Miss Bingley aside due to either of those things."

"No, you did not, but imagine, if you will, being the daughter of a wealthy tradesman. You have a fortune, but your lineage is not what is desirable. Might not those circumstances cause a lady to place herself above others?"

Richard opened his mouth and closed it again, vexation scrawled across his face.

"I may not, at this moment, like Miss Bingley," Elizabeth said, "but I can attempt to understand her. I have been contemplating such things as of late. It seems my judgments of people have at times been wanting."

Richard shook his head. "No, I reject your conclusion."

Elizabeth smiled at him. "Your acceptance or rejection does not make it either true or false."

Richard shook his head and laughed heartily. "Do you read the papers, Miss Elizabeth?"

"Occasionally."

"My father would be thrilled to have a person of your reasoning skills to debate the happenings in the world." He slapped Darcy on the back. "Again, I will repeat, I can see why Darcy is enchanted. You are as astute as you are beautiful, Miss Elizabeth," he said with a bow of his head. "However, I would beg you to feel at least a hint of compassion for me when Miss Bingley begins her barrage."

"Of course, Colonel, as long as you refute her when she disparages either me or my family."

Richard's eyes narrowed. "The way your eyes are sparkling, I fear I am being led into a trap."

Elizabeth pressed her lips together and shrugged.

"Is there a reason why Miss Bingley would disparage your family?" he asked as he extended his hand to Georgiana to lead her into dinner.

Elizabeth laughed lightly. "Being pursued by Miss Bingley may pale in comparison to being pursued by my mother. She does have five daughters to see well-matched — none with a fortune –, and she does prefer a man in uniform who is a lively conversation partner."

Richard's responding chuckle was deep, rumbling from his belly, and filled with delight. "I thank you for your warning," he said as they began to descend the stairs on their way to the dining room below.

Chapter 11

"Not be here for Christmas?" Lady Matlock repeated what Darcy had just said. "But we are always together for Christmas. It is tradition."

"I have promised my help to a friend." Darcy smiled. "Which is not the only compelling reason to be in Hertfordshire."

"But it is Christmas."

Elizabeth pulled the left corner of her lip between her teeth and looked from the man she wished to have with her in Hertfordshire and his aunt who would clearly be disappointed if he were not here, in town, at Matlock House.

"Georgiana is going with me. I do not wish to be separated from her for this holiday." Darcy reclined in his chair, cradling in his hand the glass that held what remained of his wine. He cast a glance in Richard's direction. "I have asked Richard to accompany me."

"My son? You would take my son from me at Christmas?"

"Not without good reason," Darcy said softly.

"Mr. Wickham is in Hertfordshire," Georgiana interjected.

Lady Matlock, who had been poised to protest Darcy's reason, snapped her mouth closed.

"Is it safe to take Georgie?" Viscount Wyndmere asked.

"With Richard as an escort, I see no need to fear," Darcy answered. "With any luck, just the knowledge that your brother is in Hertfordshire will send Wickham scurrying to some hole to hide." Wickham knew that, while Darcy would not call him out, Richard was not above taking such a risk or, at the at the very least, attempting to find a way within the laws of the land to make Wickham's life miserable.

The viscount allowed Darcy's answer to be true.

"Perhaps you could join Bingley after Christmas," Elizabeth offered.

"No," Georgiana said with a firm shake of her head, "that will not do."

"Are you certain?" Elizabeth asked in surprise. "I would very much dislike being the cause of a less than joyful holiday for your family. I know mine — or at least my mother's side of the family — has always gathered at Longbourn, although it is only my aunt and uncle Gardiner who have to travel to be with us."

"Not your father's family?" Viscount Wyndmere asked.

"They are estranged," Elizabeth answered. She smoothed the cloth that lay on her lap. "They did not approve of my mother." She could feel her cheeks growing warm. "Her father was a tradesman, as is my uncle Gardiner."

"Ah, so that is how you know it is just as unpleasant to be pursued for your wealth and status as it is to be cast aside for lack of the same," said Richard.

Elizabeth nodded. "My father would never admit it, but I believe he felt the disapproval quite strongly."

"Your father?" Richard asked in surprise. "I thought you were referring to your mother's not being accepted."

Elizabeth smiled. "There is that, too. However,

it is my father of whom I was speaking — not that he did not have wealth or standing but that his choice of bride did not." She looked from Richard to Darcy and tears unexpectedly gathered in her eyes. He had fled Hertfordshire because he feared being cast aside as her father had been. She blinked and lowered her eyes to her plate. "There is more on which I based my comments, I suppose. Though I am not penniless, I have no fortune, and I have ties to trade. I know that does not make me a favourable match for many."

"You are a gentleman's daughter," Lord Matlock said. "That is all that matters to me. That and how much my nephew seems to love you."

Elizabeth gave him a grateful smile as her cheeks grew rosy and his wife scolded him softly for having spoken of Darcy's feelings.

"I do love her," Darcy said, drawing the attention of the table. "However, you are speaking as if things have been settled between us. They have not, which is why I would like to spend Christmas in Hertfordshire." He glanced at his aunt. "It is not because I wish to be separated from you. It is just that I..." His voice failed him as he saw the smile that shone in Elizabeth's eyes.

"Then, you may borrow my son," his aunt replied. "Now, if everyone is finished eating, I would suggest we retire to the drawing room. You men can drink your port there. We ladies will not mind. However, you must keep your conversation to acceptable topics." She skewered her husband with a pointed look.

"Yes, my lady," he replied with a chuckle as he rose from his chair. "Darcy, see that your aunt reaches the drawing room unscathed. I should like to escort Miss Elizabeth."

Elizabeth took the earl's hand and allowed herself to be led from the room.

"We will take a turn of the drawing room while the rest are getting the card tables arranged," he said, patting her hand where it lay on his arm. "I would like to meet your father."

"You would?" Elizabeth asked in surprise.

"Yes, I would like to meet both your father and the rest of your family."

They took several silent steps before he asked, "Why do you look so troubled?"

Elizabeth, who had been pondering her mother's exuberant response to meeting an earl and her younger sister's giggling, blew out a breath. "I am not a good match for him."

"I beg your pardon?"

"My lord, along with having no fortune and ties to trade, my family is not what it should be."

He turned her from the card tables and led her back into the hall. "I feel we are not ready to pick up our cards yet," he explained. "Please, continue. I am very much interested in why you feel your family is not what it should be."

"Mr. Darcy is so...so..." she paused, searching for the right word, "dignified. He has been raised to greatness." She shook her head. "I have not."

"That tells me nought of your family," Lord Matlock prodded.

"My father's estate is modest. It produces well, but, I am nearly certain, it could produce better." She sighed. "And my mother." She shook her head. "I love her, but she is not always sensible, and my younger sisters are rather silly because of it." She shook her head again. "He could do far better than me."

"I see," Lord Matlock said as they reached the end of the hall and turned to make the return trip to the drawing room. However, instead of continuing to walk, he stopped and motioned to a couch that stood along the wall under a beautiful painting of an outdoor scene. "It may come as a surprise to you, Miss Elizabeth, but my mother was not the most sensible woman either. She would prattle on for hours about the most inane things and insist on the most absurd strictures at times. I had two sisters. Darcy's mother, Anne, was sweet as could be and not at all like my mother. However, my sister Catherine is the very image of our mother. And my brother?" He grimaced and shook his head. "He was happy to go to sea to be away from both Catherine and our mother. He was sensible to a fault at times and yet unyieldingly foolish at others."

He covered her hand with his. "When my sister discovers Darcy is marrying you." He held up a hand to stop her protest. "I realize you are not yet betrothed, but you will be," he assured her with a squeeze of her hand. "As I was saying, when Catherine realizes that Darcy is not marrying her daughter, she will likely put on a demonstration that would make anything your mother could do pale in comparison. She has said for years that Darcy would marry Anne, and no matter how many times, Darcy's parents or I, myself, refuted it, she would not listen." He smiled. "Did I mention she is not always sensible?"

Elizabeth nodded. Darcy's uncle was a surprisingly easy person with whom to speak. She felt as at ease sitting her with him as she did her own uncle.

"I say all this, Miss Elizabeth, to assure you that your family will not offend me."

"And what of my ties to trade?"

"You are a gentleman's daughter."

"But my uncle and aunt are very dear to me."

"Do you fear not being permitted to see them?"

She shrugged. "I had thought all gentleman, especially those with titles, wanted nothing to do with men of trade."

He squeezed her hand again and smiled. "And what is Bingley? Besides a most amiable man and Darcy's particular friend? He is not yet a gentleman, is he?"

A smile spread across her face as she laughed lightly at her own foolishness.

"In addition to that, my brother did not go to see on a naval ship but on a merchant one. He is in India." He chuckled. "I see I have shocked you.

It was quite the scandal." He stood and drew her to her feet. "Miss Elizabeth," he said as they began walking, "I will be delighted if you chose to join your family with mine. Darcy deserves to be loved. That is the only requirement that I will leave with you to consider when you are deciding whether or not to accept his offer when he finally gets around to making it. If you do not love him, then you are not a good match for him. However, if you do love him, then there can be no better match." He patted her hand. "Are we agreed?"

"Yes." Again, Elizabeth pondered that word love as she had in her aunt's sitting room earlier today. "Then, " she said softly as her heart beat a loud and rapid rhythm in her chest, "I am a good match for him."

"I am glad to hear it," Lord Matlock said with another pat for Elizabeth's hand. "Ah, see, I knew it would happen." He chuckled and nodded toward the drawing room door from which Darcy had just exited. "I knew he would come looking for you," he whispered to Elizabeth. Then, raising his voice as Darcy approached, he said, "I can see my services are no longer needed." He lifted Elizabeth's hand from his arm and held it out to Darcy. "We can play a person or two short. Take a walk. Show her the library."

Darcy looked uncertainly from Elizabeth to his uncle.

Lord Matlock shrugged. "Leave the door open if you must." He smiled at Elizabeth. "I think Miss Elizabeth could use a few more minutes to collect herself after our discussion." He clapped Darcy on the shoulder and took his leave.

"Are you well?" Darcy asked as they walked toward the grand staircase.

"I am."

"The library is just behind the dining room," he explained to Elizabeth as they began descending the stairs. "You do not mind going there do you?" He glanced at her. He did not wish to put her in a place where she was uncomfortable, no matter what his uncle suggested.

"No, I love libraries."

"But we are unaccompanied."

Elizabeth's cheeks coloured, and she carefully watched where she was walking. "We were given permission." She peeked up at him. "Would you rather not go to the library? We can return to the drawing room."

He shook his head. "I would always much rather go to the library than the drawing room," he said with a smile. "The library here is among my favourite rooms."

"Is it? Pray tell, which other rooms are on your list of favourites?" she teased.

"The library at Darcy House, the library at Pemberley, and the library at Netherfield."

She laughed. "Do you enjoy any rooms that are not libraries?"

He shrugged. "My study both at Pemberley and Darcy House are quite comfortable, as are my rooms in both places."

"No drawing rooms?" There was a teasing tone to her voice.

"I do not mind them, but if I had to choose between a drawing room filled with people and a well-stocked library, I would choose the library. I am not well-versed in the art of conversation. It is not something that comes easily to me."

"I do not believe that for a moment," Elizabeth retorted. Her breath caught and whatever she was going to add to her rebuttal was snatched from her mind as she glimpsed the sight which lay beyond the door he was opening. "Oh, how beautiful!"

"You see why it is a favourite then?"

"Indeed, I do!"

Two walls were lined with shelves of books which reached from the floor to the ceiling. One set of shelves was interrupted by a door that Darcy told her led to his uncle's study while the other vast expanse of volumes was broken up by two windows evenly spaced. On the far end of the room and only a short distance from the door to Lord Matlock's study, was a grouping of two chairs and a small sofa with a low table standing before a fireplace. In the midst of the room, were more chairs, a table, a globe, and a few other cabinets and furnishings, all neatly arranged.

"This," Darcy said as he led her toward the fireplace, "is my favourite place to sit. Richard and I have spent a great deal of time in discussions here." He smiled at the memory. "Uncle Henry often joins us and shares his wisdom. Chair or sofa?" He had stopped in front of the sofa and wished to pull her down onto it beside him, but he could not bring himself to be so presumptuous.

"The sofa will be perfect," she replied with a smile. "It is where you wished to sit, is it not?"

"It is," he admitted. "I had hoped you would sit with me."

"And I shall." She took a seat and gave the cushion on her right a pat, inviting him to be seated.

"Before we entered, you said you did not believe I struggle with conversation." He had always felt awkward in drawing rooms — a fact that was painfully obvious to all on many occasions. Therefore, he was curious to hear her explanation of her claim.

"You converse very well, sir, when you are at ease," she said with a smile. "Why, today, at my aunt's house, you did not stumble once, and I would venture a guess that you rarely are without something to say when at Mrs. Verity's. The children would not be so comfortable around you if you were not also comfortable. And this evening, you have carried on a great deal of conversation both in the dining room and the drawing room. Therefore, I suggest that it is not conversation skills which you lack, but rather the ability to feel at ease in unfamiliar places and with unfamiliar people."

He shook his head as a smile spread across his face. She was right, of course. If he looked at it as she was, he had to admit it was a lack of feeling at ease that seemed to tie his tongue. "While I will allow you to be correct, I cannot say you have been completely thorough in your evaluation."

"Have I not?" Her knee brushed against his leg as she turned toward him.

"No," he said, taking her hand. "There are people such as my aunt Catherine who are not strange to me, nor is her house unfamiliar, yet I am as unable to speak in her presence as I was at the assembly in Meryton. I fear I am rather arrogant when I am at Rosings."

"She makes you uneasy?"

He nodded. "She is demanding, and she expects me to marry my cousin." His brows furrowed, and his eyes filled with concern as he mentioned it. "I am not betrothed to her."

"I know. Lord Matlock told me, but," her gaze dropped to the hand that was clasped in his, "I had already heard of your betrothal from both my cousin, Mr. Collins, and Mr. Wickham."

"And yet you have given me leave to call on you without asking me if it was true?"

She looked up at him. "It was not true. I knew that." Her eyes dropped to her hand again. "After hearing your sister's tale when she called and then learning what you did for Nellie and the others at Mrs. Verity's there was absolutely no trace of doubt about your character left in my mind. You are among the best of men. You would not call on one lady while being promised to another."

"I would not place myself there," he said, though his heart thrilled to hear her say it, he still felt woefully inadequate at times, especially when he considered Georgiana's ordeal.

"That is just it," she replied. "The best of men never place themselves in such a category. The scoundrels and rouges attempt it, but never those who truly deserve such a title."

"Thank you," he whispered, unsure of what else to say to such a thing.

"I apologise. I have made you uncomfortable."

He looked at her in surprise. How did she know that?

"You have fallen silent," she whispered.

He chuckled. "I have, have I not? And now, when my heart is so full that it feels as if it will burst from my chest." He lifted her hand and brushed his lips against her knuckles. "I cannot express to you how delighted I am to hear I have won your good opinion. You have long had mine, but it deepens upon each meeting. You are the most handsome lady I have ever met, and not just because of your beauty. Your heart, your integrity, your truthfulness, all that is you cannot now or ever be overshone by another." He lifted her chin to raise her eyes, which had once again lowered to look at her hand, and gazed for a brief moment on her flushed cheeks and her eyes that shone with happiness.

"I love you and would like to speak to your father when I am in Hertfordshire." He cupped her rosy cheek in his hand. "Do I have your permission to ask him for your hand?"

A smile spread across her face as she nodded her consent.

"You would have me?"

Again, she nodded. "If you will have me."

"I should like nothing better," he replied. There was one more thing he wished to know. "Do you love me?"

"Yes," she replied before he could even draw an anxious breath.

"You love me." The words settled in around his

heart, wrapping it in a comforting peace he had never before felt.

She nodded. "Very much. So very, very much."

She loved him. The words proclaimed themselves loudly in his mind. She loved him. "May I kiss you?" he asked in a voice that was barely above a whisper.

She saw the longing in his eyes as well as the uncertainty. Such a loving look could not be met with anything less than a willing acquiescence.

Leaning forward, he gently brushed her lips with his. Then, pausing to make certain she was not startled or uneasy, he whispered, "I love you," before claiming her lips in a kiss that both left no doubt in her mind as to the truth of his words and compelled her to respond in kind.

Chapter 12

Georgiana draped her pelisse over the back of a chair and placed her gloves, hat, and reticule on the table beside it. Everything else had been stored away in her travelling case or was tucked under the seat in the carriage just waiting for their departure. Excitement and fear warred within her as she anticipated her trip to Netherfield.

"I am afraid my brother is not home," she said after greeting the people gathered in the drawing room. "However, I do expect him to return at any moment."

"Oh, I am certain we can wait as long as needed," Caroline Bingley said sweetly.

Before stepping into the drawing room, Georgiana had heard Caroline complaining to her brother about having to wait.

"I am sure you are anxious to return to Netherfield," Mrs. Annesley said.

Caroline raised a disapproving brow at the mere servant who deigned to speak and made no reply.

Georgiana bristled at the dismissive action. "I know I am all anticipation at the prospect of finally seeing Netherfield. I have heard so much about it." Indeed, she had heard plenty about the rooms and gardens from Jane, Elizabeth, and Bingley with a smattering of details thrown in by her brother. Of course, most of the things he mentioned, such as the library, were for Bingley to consider as needing improvement. Once Fitzwilliam had renewed his determination to see his friend well-settled in an estate, he had taken it upon himself to draw up a list of items to which he thought Bingley should see.

Bingley had been eager to listen and learn, of course, while Jane and Elizabeth had preferred to answer Georgiana's questions about the more homely items of furnishing and fabrics.

"You will simply adore it," Caroline cooed.

"Do you?" Georgiana asked pointedly.

"Do I adore Netherfield?" Caroline asked with wide eyes.

"Yes. Do you adore Netherfield? I know that Miss Bennet and Miss Elizabeth both speak highly of it, but until this moment, I have not heard you praise it at all."

Caroline lifted her chin. "You have not been home to callers enough for me to speak to you about such things." The bitterness in her voice was plain to all.

"I do apologize, but I have been out."

A sour look settled on Caroline's face. "Of course." She sighed. "Miss Bennet and Miss Elizabeth have very little with which to compare Netherfield, so they will naturally be more impressed than I am. I have seen Pemberley after all, and Pemberley is an estate without an equal. Be that as it may, Netherfield's gardens are appropriately sized and styled. They are neither grand nor ostentatious. They are appropriate to the grandeur of the house and do not detract from it."

Georgiana smiled and muttered her agreement that simple, dignified gardens were what she preferred.

"The house is impressive. There are none that outshine it in the immediate area. The next largest home is Longbourn." Her lips curled in derision.

"And Longbourn is of no great beauty. It has a very small park and," she shook her head and lowered her voice, "it is not well-tended."

"Caroline," Bingley snapped. "Longbourn is a fine estate. It is not so large as Netherfield, but I will not have you disparaging our neighbours."

Caroline's lips pursed and her eyes narrowed. "Our neighbours are much like their estate — of no great beauty and not very well-tended. The youngest Bennets!" She shook her head. "And their mother! I do not know why you would wish to tie yourself to such a family."

"Indeed?" Georgiana's brows rose as she turned amused eyes to Bingley. Bingley had mentioned how his sister was not pleased about returning to Netherfield or his plans to marry Jane — he had already acquired Mr. Bennet's permission and was merely waiting to make his offer and present her with his fede ring. But it was surprising to hear Caroline speak so freely.

"Are they so bad? My brother has not said they are." She knew how Bingley and her brother had described the rest of the Bennet family as well as the cautioning that Elizabeth had given her about her mother and sisters.

"Enthusiastic, a touch unrefined, but pleasant," he responded with a glare for his sister. "And well enough bred to not speak of their neighbours in such a demeaning fashion, but then, you are not a gentleman's daughter, so perhaps that is why your civility is lacking?"

Caroline huffed.

Georgiana's eyes grew wide at Bingley's open and harsh reprimand.

"Civility is not a mark of birth but of character," Mrs. Annesley added, drawing a look of absolute loathing from Caroline.

"My brother should be returning soon," Georgiana repeated. "He had a particular errand to which he needed to attend."

Caroline huffed again. "I cannot see why we must wait while he calls on orphans."

"Because it is nearly Christmas, and he will not be in town to see it done on that day," Georgiana replied. "Ah, here he is." Darcy had stepped into the room with Elizabeth on his arm. Elizabeth was to join Georgiana, Richard, and Darcy in their carriage, while Jane travelled with the Gardiners to assist with the children.

"I am afraid I have one more task that needs my

attention," he said. "I will be no longer than five minutes. Has our cousin arrived?"

"No. But he knew you would be busy this morning and likely adjusted his time accordingly." It was not like Richard to be late for an appointment, nor was it like him to arrive early when there were people such as Miss Bingley whom he wished to avoid. Georgiana was curious to see how he would avoid her while at Netherfield.

True to his word, Darcy was only five minutes and had his cousin at his heels. "Richard was in the kitchen," he explained, seeing Georgiana's questioning look. "He was pilfering biscuits and teasing the maids." He shook his head but smiled, letting one and all know that he was not displeased. "It seems the servant's entrance is not guarded well enough."

"Perhaps if your lions roared instead of meowing, they would be more fearsome," Richard quipped as one of those more-friendly-than-fearsome creatures wound its way around his legs.

"They do love you," Georgiana said with a laugh.

"It is because he brings them fish," Darcy assured her. "A few scraps each time he calls."

"I will not have to smell fish all the way to Hertfordshire, will I?" Georgiana asked Richard.

He shook his head and winked at her. "They also appreciate a morsel of cheese now and again."

"If you spoil them too much, they shall not catch the mice as they are supposed to do," Georgiana scolded.

Richard bent and scratched the ear of the tabby that was still weaving around and through his legs. "They know their duty. We have discussed it, have we not, Hattie?"

The cat replied with a meow.

"See?" Richard said with a laugh.

"Are we ready then?" Darcy asked.

"We are," Georgiana rose and allowed Richard to help her with her pelisse. "The blankets and foot warmers are waiting in the carriage as is a tin of biscuits and a few rolls and cheese. Did the children enjoy their gifts even if they were two days early?"

"They did," Darcy replied.

"Gifts? You were giving gifts to orphans?" Caroline Bingley paused at the door to the sitting room.

"No," Darcy said with a shake of his head as he extended a hand to Elizabeth, "*We* were giving gifts to *children*. It is a tradition that I began about five years ago, and it is one Miss Elizabeth and I intend to continue."

Georgiana was almost certain that Caroline Bingley was about to swoon as she looked from Darcy to Elizabeth and back. "And why would Miss Elizabeth be carrying on this tradition?" she asked in a strained whisper.

"Has your brother not told you?" Darcy made a show of removing Elizabeth's glove from her left hand as Elizabeth blushed and smiled prettily. "Last week, I asked Miss Elizabeth to be my wife. Two days ago, because I could not wait until we arrived in Hertfordshire to do it, I persuaded her father to accept me, and today, I presented her with my mother's ring." He showed the small gold band inset with diamonds and amethysts to them all.

"I had meant to keep it until Christmas, but Master Riley would not be in Hertfordshire to see it, and he will be gone from Mrs. Verity's after Christmas." His smile was broad as he continued. "I have just informed the household to expect a new mistress in the new year." He allowed Elizabeth to replace her glove. "They are assembling to see us off," he said to her softly.

"Well, we do not need a send-off," said Richard,

looking at Bingley and nodding toward the door to indicate they should leave.

Bingley willingly scooted out the door, taking Caroline with him.

"Georgie," Richard called from the doorway.

"In a moment," Georgiana replied.

Richard sighed and leaned against the doorframe to wait.

"I know I said this last week at Matlock House, but I am so delighted," she gave Elizabeth a hug and then turned to her brother and took his hands. "I know I have a parcel tucked away for you in my bag, but this," she reached over and taking Elizabeth's hand, placed it on top of her brother's, "this is my Christmas gift."

Darcy's brows furrowed, and he glanced at Elizabeth, who merely shrugged and shook her head letting him know that she was just as confused as he.

"You saved me from misery when you arrived in Ramsgate, and when I saw you return from Netherfield in such a state of despondency, I vowed I would find a way to save you from misery — a different sort of misery to be sure, but misery just the same." She squeezed the hands that she held wrapped in her own. "I had thought it would be more challenging. I had considered scheming my way to Hertfordshire and pleading your case with Miss Elizabeth." She shook her head. "I did not know if I could succeed in sparing your heart from being broken, but I knew I had to try, in some small way, to repay you for how you have cared for mine." She released her hold on their hands. "I am pleased that it has worked out as it has." She expelled a breath as her brother wrapped her in his embrace.

"Thank you," he whispered and kissed the top of her head. "I could not ask for a better gift."

She placed a gloved hand on his cheek. "No, you could not," she replied with an impertinent grin.

He rolled his eyes and laughed as she left the room. "Are you ready to be greeted by what will soon be your new household staff?" he asked Elizabeth as he brushed a tear from her cheek.

"Your sister...," she said as another tear slid down her cheek.

"She is rather wonderful, is she not?"

Elizabeth nodded.

"Come. We must go," he said, drying her eyes with his handkerchief. "There are celebrations and a new life awaiting us in Hertfordshire." He cupped her face in his hands. "There truly is no better gift she could have given me," he said before bending to kiss her softly.

Elizabeth could not agree more. Darcy's love was the best Christmas gift she could have ever received, and every year, from that one forward, in addition to gifts being exchanged on Christmas morning in the Darcy home, gifts of the heart would be given as well. But these gifts, these special gifts of love, would neither be given nor received on Christmas morning but would always be shared, just as Georgiana's had been — two days before Christmas.

~*~*~

Coming January 2018:

One Winter's Eve, a sequel to *Two Day's Before Christmas*, which will tell the story of how Elizabeth's challenge to Colonel Fitzwilliam to reconsider his opinion of Caroline Bingley plays a part in altering the course of his life

Before You Go

If you enjoyed this book, be sure to let others know by leaving a review.

~*~*~

Always know what's new with Leenie's books by subscribing to her mailing list and as a thank you, you will receive a copy of *Teatime Tales* as well as *Better Than She Deserved, A Willow Hall Romance Sequel:*

Book News from Leenie Brown

(http://eepurl.com/bS1eI1)

Acknowledgements

There are many who have had a part in the creation of this story. Some have read and commented on it. Some have proofread for grammatical errors and plot holes. Others have not even read the story and a few, I know, never will. However, their encouragement and belief in my ability, as well as their patience when I became cranky or when supper was late or the groceries ran low, was invaluable.

And so, I would like to say *thank you* to Zoe, Rose, Kristine, Ben, and Kyle. I feel blessed by your help, support, and understanding.

I have not listed my dear husband in the above group because, to me, he deserves his own special thank you, for, without his somewhat pushy insistence that I start sharing my writing, none of my writing goals and dreams would have been realized.

Leenie B Books

Novels ~ Novellas ~ Shorts

~*~

Oxford Cottage: A Pride and Prejudice Variation

For Peace of Mind: A Pride and Prejudice Variation

Teatime Tales: Six Short and Sweet Austen-Inspired Stories

Listen To Your Heart: A Pride and Prejudice Variation

With the Colonel's Help: A Pride and Prejudice Novella

Two Days before Christmas: A Pride and Prejudice Novella

Coming January 2018:

One Winter's Eve: A Sequel to Two Days before Christmas

~*~

The Choices Series: Pride & Prejudice Novellas (available as a bundle and individually)

Her Father's Choice (book 1)

No Other Choice (book 2)

His Inconvenient Choice (book 3)

Her Heart's Choice (book 4)

~*~

A Dash of Darcy Collection

Finally Mrs. Darcy: A Pride and Prejudice Novella

Waking to Mr. Darcy: A Pride and Prejudice Novella

Discovering Mr.Darcy: A Pride and Prejudice Novella

Unravelling Mr. Darcy: A Pride and Prejudice Novella

~*~

A Dash of Darcy Companion Story Collection

A Very Merry Christmas: A Pride and Prejudice Novella (*A sequel to Waking to Mr. Darcy*)

Not an Heiress: A Pride and Prejudice Novella (*A sequel to Discovering Mr. Darcy*)

Becoming Entangled: A Pride and Prejudice Novella (*A sequel to Unravelling* Mr. *Darcy*)

~*~

Willow Hall Romances

And Then Love: A Pride and Prejudice Variation Prequel (book 1)

The Tenant's Guest: A Pride and Prejudice Variation Novella (book 2)

So Very Unexpected: A Pride and Prejudice Variation Novel (book3)

At All Costs: A Pride and Prejudice Variation Novel (book 4)

Better Than She Deserved: A Pride and Prejudice Novelette (sequel 1)

~*~

Touches of Austen Collection

His Beautiful Bea

~*~

Other Pens

Through Every Storm: A Pride and Prejudice Novella

Henry: To Prove Himself Worthy (*A Mansfield Park Continuation*)

About the Author

Leenie Brown has always been a girl with an active imagination, which, while growing up, was a both an asset, providing many hours of fun as she played out stories, and a liability, when her older sister and aunt would tell her frightening tales. At one time, they had her convinced Dracula lived in the trunk at the end of the bed she slept in when visiting her grandparents!

Although it has been years since she cowered in her bed in her grandparents' basement, she still has an imagination which occasionally runs away with her, and she feeds it now as she did then — by reading!

Her heroes, when growing up, were authors, and the worlds they painted with words were (and still are) her favourite playgrounds! Now, as an adult, she spends much of her time in the Regency world, playing with the characters from her favourite Jane Austen novels and those of her own creation.

When she is not traipsing down a trail in an attempt to keep up with her imagination, Leenie resides in the beautiful province of Nova Scotia with her two sons and her very own Mr. Brown (a wonderful mix of all the best of Darcy, Bingley, and Edmund with a healthy dose of the teasing Mr. Tilney and just a dash of the scolding Mr. Knightley).

Connect with Leenie Brown

E-mail:

LeenieBrownAuthor@gmail.com

Facebook:

www.facebook.com/LeenieBrownAuthor

Blog:

leeniebrown.com

Patreon:

https://www.patreon.com/LeenieBrown

Subscribe to Leenie's Mailing List:

Book News from Leenie Brown

(http://eepurl.com/bS1eI1)

Join Leenie on Austen Authors:

austenauthors.net

Made in the USA
Monee, IL
12 November 2022

17625921R00115